THE CERES ILLUSION

SUE EATON

Cover design copyright © 2023 by Niki Lenhart
nikilen-designs.com

Published by Water Dragon Publishing
waterdragonpublishing.com

ISBN 978-1-962538-04-6 (Trade Paperback)

10 9 8 7 6 5 4 3 2 1

FIRST EDITION

*This book is for Miss Bird, my second-year teacher,
who taught me how to string words together to make stories.*

ACKNOWLEDGMENTS

I'd like to thank The Renegade Writers Group for pulling this apart while giving me ideas for putting it back together.

Thanks also go to Water Dragon Publishing for having faith in me.

THE CERES ILLUSION

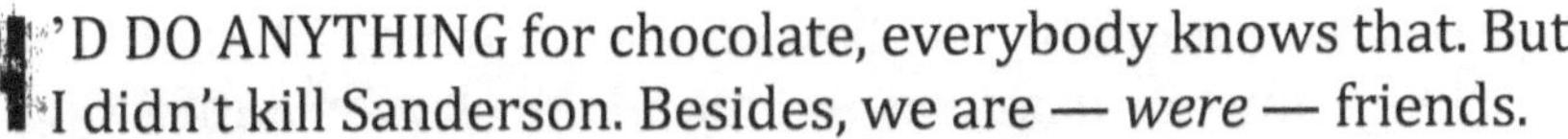

I'D DO ANYTHING for chocolate, everybody knows that. But I didn't kill Sanderson. Besides, we are — *were* — friends.

Sanderson lived in the apartment next to me, and as we worked in the same building we usually walked to the monopod together, but yesterday morning he didn't answer my call. I knocked on his door and, when he didn't answer, I walked in as I would normally do, calling out in case he was doing something I didn't need to see.

The smell hit me first: foul, fecal and with an underlying coppery odor. While I was trying to place it, I was horrified to discover a mess of blood and tissue with Sanderson's head lying at a funny angle on his living room floor. He was staring at me as if to say, "Help me, please."

That was the expression, not terrified as you would think, just helpless. Strange, as someone or something had ripped him to shreds. I didn't believe what I was seeing, and I certainly don't believe that anyone here did that. I shook for hours afterwards and ate some of his chocolate because I'm told sugar is good for shock.

Sanderson and I, along with Big John, better known as BJ, have been friends since I can remember. Of course, we fight and fall out, only to become friends again. Sometimes we can do that all in one day, but we would never hurt each other. Not intentionally, and not seriously.

I am the only one apart from the Security Enforcement Team who saw it and they were quick to push me out and shut the door. Did I call them? I must have, or how had they known? I can't remember calling them, but then, I was in shock. I have been questioned by the Head of the Team and then let go. She didn't even hint that she thought I might have done it. In fact, she seemed eager to get rid of me. I was allowed the day off from work with the order to rest. In some ways I would have liked to have gone in, for the company, but I doubt I would have been much use. I mean, if Sanderson could be torn to shreds in the relative safety of his own apartment without anyone hearing a thing, it stands to reason that I could be too. It is not a comforting thought.

I kept my television on, as I found the chatter comforting, but it's not been on the newsfeed. The fact that he's dead has not been acknowledged by anyone.

•   •   •

Today is a rest day and I am sitting on the steps outside of the apartment building Sanderson and I live in — *I* live in. I don't understand why the attack's not been on the newsfeed. It happened yesterday afternoon and things are usually broadcast immediately. I can understand them not wanting to upset morale. Everything seems to revolve around morale here. It's *don't do that it will upset morale*, or *you must do this in order to boost morale*. Living my life the way I want to would boost *my* morale far more than following the petty rules of the community. But we need to know what's going on and we need to stay alert; on the lookout for anything strange. Goodness knows where it will end if something isn't done about it.

BJ comes by this afternoon before tea. "What's to do, Jax?" he wants to know.

"Just thinking," I tell him.

"What'yu thinking, Jax?"

"About Sanderson."

"What about Sanderson? He's gone." As if that was the end of anything to do with him.

"Doesn't that upset you?"

"Dunno." He sits down beside me on the step.

"He was our friend. I'm still shaking — look." I hold out a quivering hand. He doesn't look, not really.

"So?"

BJ hadn't seen what I had seen, but we were friends with Sanderson. Surely, he must feel something. I appreciate that in the main, people in the domes are reserved to the point of being frigid, but small friendship groups form, usually around a common interest. I know of no other way of living to compare it to. I feel the loss, so shouldn't BJ?

"What about his family?" I ask.

"What about them?"

"Have they been informed?"

"Dunno." BJ doesn't sound as if he really cares.

"Surely, they'll come for this."

"They might have a long way to come."

"Hardly. I know they must be in another dome, but they aren't that far away it takes a day to get here."

"I mean, they might be on Earth for all we know," BJ suggests.

"Hardly," I comment. Our parents were among the founder members sent out to inhabit this rather inhospitable lump of rock, and they all came from the Martian colony, not Earth. Earth is a bit of a dump these days, allegedly.

I suddenly realise that we rarely speak about our past. It is as if we have only the vaguest memories of our earlier lives. We know we have parents, we've been told about them, but everyone talks in generic terms, like, our families came from Mars. Not my mum or my dad, but our families. Once we finish our schooling, we are moved from our families and set to work. There are only young people in my dome, DN 2, and all are workers. I suppose you could call it a dormitory dome. There's always talk about visits, but I don't ever remember anyone visiting and I have never been on a visit. I have likenesses of my family to help me remember, but I have to keep them hidden. A thought crosses my mind and I ask, "Where are your parents, BJ?"

"DN ... er ... I can't remember the dome number, but they are here."

"My ... mmm." I had been about to say that my parents lived in DN — but then find that I can't remember either. I have a brother, I think. I have a likeness of one anyway.

In fact, Sanderson is fading from my memory and I have to keep worrying at it to keep it sharp.

"Work tomorrow," muses BJ.

"It'll be strange without Sanderson."

"Who?" BJ is busy inspecting a nail.

See what I mean? I stand and shove my hands into my jacket pockets, feeling the remains of the chocolate as I do so. I decide then and there to go to the Security Enforcement Office in our dome at the first opportunity. I am curious as to why the story's not been on the newsfeed. I look at BJ. He is chewing his fingernails with an absent look on his face. Gormless lummox. I will go on my own.

•   •   •

"Who did you say you were looking for?" The Enforcement Officer stares at me, making me uncomfortable, but I will not back down.

"I'm not looking for anyone," I tell him. "My friend who lived in the apartment next to mine was killed yesterday and I'm wondering how the investigation is going."

"Who would that be then?" He doesn't even look at the technopad on his desk. He could at least pretend to be interested.

"7:5/1 Sanderson, Jaimz."

"Where does he live?"

"RN-10, T-2." We use initials for everything. Translated that means Room Number 10, Tower 2.

"I can only deal with things that happen in this dome," the Officer tells me with a straight face.

"It *is* in this dome. Sir, how many murders do you have on your books?" Perhaps I should be more respectful, but I am getting annoyed with his attitude.

"Don't you be cheeky, young madam. We have no murders. What are you talking about? I thought you'd lost your friend?"

"Yes, to *murder*," I emphasize. "I'm worried."

"Don't know anything about that. Why don't you ask your friend?"

"He's dead and I'm scared someone else might be next."

"You're scared? About what?"

"About being the next one to be attacked." Is he being deliberately obtrusive?

"Attacked? Who was attacked?"

"Sanderson."

"Sanderson? Who's that?"

"... Oh never mind. I'll ask my friends."

"Should have done that in the first place, young lady. Have a nice day."

I stamp out as belligerently as I dare and don't see what he does next.

THE CERES DAY is very short — nine Earth hours and a couple of minutes if you're being really pedantic — but within the domes we keep to the times of our mother planet, which we still consider to be the Earth despite our ancestors having established themselves on Mars hundreds of years ago.

The day is highly structured, the premise being that if you are busy you won't get into mischief. Rumor has it that when the domes were set up and the artificial timing was programmed into the system, the leader of the early settlers wanted to decimalize the day but was overruled in favor of tradition. So, we have the regulation twenty-four hours in each cycle: eight hours work, eight hours sleep and eight hours to do as we will from a specified list. Structured. Artificial lighting denotes the hour and there seem to be clocks everywhere encouraging us not to waste a second. We live by the chimes and the chirpy little voices that tell us where we should be in order to have *a nice day*. I could cheerfully blast them from the walls.

The artificial sun is still shining as I leave the S E Office and I am free until the next morning. I decide to see if I can get into Sanderson's rooms. He might have some information stashed there about a life I am not aware of. I can't be the only one with secrets.

I wander as aimlessly as I can into the foyer of my apartment block. They are called towers, but they are not overly tall, just four levels and all identical. I live on the top floor.

I take the elevator to my floor. There is no one about, and from the look of the corridor, you would not believe a cruel murder took place there yesterday. I pass my door and lean against Sanderson's. There is nothing to indicate that no one should enter, and as I've had no experience of crime scenes, I think nothing of it. There is little to no crime within the colony; no one really owns anything, as all essentials are government issue and not worth stealing. You can just help yourself from the stores. Most people never lock their doors, despite having DNA recognition pads for security.

Sanderson's door gives under my weight, and I slip inside. There is nothing in the room to suggest anyone has ever lived there. It is clean and has that new material smell. The carpet in the living area is new. There is no blood stain, which is understandable. The walls have been repainted in an immaculate pale colour and the blood splatters have all gone.

I walk further in. Sanderson had spilt some cherrysynthe, his favorite flavor of soda, only the other day in the kitchen area. He had not managed to get the stain out completely and the maintenance 'bot had not replaced the floor covering. I can see no stain; the tiled floor has either been super-cleaned or replaced. I peek into the bedroom and see that the bed is not made up; the bedding, new and neatly folded, is sitting at one end waiting. The closets and cupboards are empty, doors and drawers open waiting to receive somebody's belongings. Everything looks new and unused.

I touch my chest and dig into my memory. Am I right about the stain? I know I am because the drink had splashed onto my shoes and is still there. I can just make out the pale pink mark despite the cleaning. I focus on the mark in my mind and drag the memories back. I don't think I will find out what happened to Sanderson.

I am deep in thought when I hear the faint whirr of the elevator. For some reason I feel it better if I am not found in a room that is not only not my own, but also so recently the scene of a dreadful murder. I glide out and onto the landing. I am standing outside my apartment door when the lift doors open, and a janitor steps out. It is dragging a house-keeping trolley. It stares towards me before disappearing into Sanderson's room, leaving the door open.

"Hello?" I inquire.

"State your query."

Bloody robots, so pedantic.

"Why are you here now?"

"We have an occupant arriving. Tonight." Clipped and to the point.

"Who's that then?"

"That is not part of my need-to-know."

"Sorry. Just curious."

"Killed the cat. You need to beware curiosity."

I feel a jolt. I have heard that saying before. I touch my chest, as the likenesses of my family are hidden in my clothes. My mum used to say it when I wouldn't leave something alone. I don't remember it properly; I just feel that she said it.

"It's just — well, I'll be living next door."

"You should be at your work or your hobby." It turns to stare at me. I can hear the electrodes whirring. Janitors are just basic models, nothing fancy.

"On my way. Good-night." I dive into my own room before I am tempted to ask any more awkward questions. I do not see the new occupant arrive.

•　　•　　•

My hobby has landed me in trouble. Just the once — there are no second chances here. Life is precarious, and if you don't follow the rules, you could jeopardize the whole colony. You are informed that your behavior is incorrect, and if you don't change it immediately, you suffer the sanction. It is not done graciously.

I like drawing, particularly people. I can get a good likeness without too much effort. Here, drawing is an acceptable hobby, providing it is of still life or landscape. Portraits and recognizable people in landscapes apparently are not, as I found out to my cost. I had all my work confiscated one afternoon. It is the one memory I can recall with any degree of clarity.

I was called to the office of our Lead Educator one afternoon. This event was unusual. No-one looked up from their screens as I rose from my console, but the atmosphere was electric. Something was amiss and everyone was agog as to what I had done.

That's how you think, isn't it? If you are called out without being given a reason, everyone, including yourself, presumes it's because you have done something wrong. Praise is given openly in front of everyone.

Two important-looking people stood without movement behind the Lead Educator when I entered the office. They were dressed in identical uniforms of a kind I had not seen before and looked very stern. They offered no greeting or even eye contact. One held a folio. Every pupil who had chosen art as their hobby had one, all exactly the same, but I knew this was mine. We had personalized our book covers as only teenagers can. It was mine. The Lead Educator looked pale and frightened, but greeted me cordially.

It could only have been seconds, but it seemed that we waited for an age in silence. I could feel the blood burning in my face even though I didn't know what I could possibly have done that was so wrong. At some signal, unseen by me, the uniformed woman opened the folio and took out some of the papers. They were drawings of my friends; caricatures I had drawn to entertain them during some spare time one afternoon recess. She passed them to the man, one at a time and he tore them into tiny little pieces before opening his hands and letting them drift, amidst the silence, to spiral to the floor.

When the last had been torn to nothing the woman shut the folio with a slap. The man spoke for the first and only time. "No more." They turned and left in silence, and I was standing red-faced in front of the Lead Educator.

Softly as if she was afraid of being overheard she whispered, "I didn't realize you were so good at drawing." I still stood with my head down, cheeks burning. Louder this time, she instructed, "Please clear up the mess 5:6/1. Jacqueline LeBrun. Then take your folio and don't do any more likenesses in the future."

A suction 'bot stood in the corner of the room, waiting. I quickly ordered it to clean up the pieces, but when I picked up my folio I felt a sharp stab in my middle finger. I dropped the folder and jabbed the finger into my mouth, tasting copper and something else I couldn't place. As the pain receded, I grabbed my work and with my head high I went back to my lesson. I remember it all so vividly. Did they do something to me? Is that why I remember the incident so clearly? I was, and am still, too scared to contemplate it further.

Did I stop drawing faces? Of course not. I thought of hiding them under my mattress, but the two strangers had scared me sufficiently that I have kept only five, and I hid them where no one would dare to look without the proper authorization in triplicate. I have five tiny portraits that I keep in my brassiere at all times. The latest one is of Sanderson, and when I take it out and look at it, I remember him. I cannot remember the other people I was at school with, apart from Big John and the few who live and work near me. People I see every day.

No-one mentioned the incident afterwards, but I cannot forget it. I carried on with art as my chosen hobby, but now I concentrate on intricate close-up details of the flora that has been introduced under the domes. I hope it will keep the *powers-that-be* off my back.

It was shortly after this incident that I realized there were no stored likenesses or recognizable images of people, despite everything else we did being recorded. There are no cameras recording people's movements. This is an experimental colony, and as such we are reviewed on a regular basis, everything we do is tracked and commented on. Feelings are analyzed and preferences recorded. I don't know how they know all about us for our reviews, but they do. All data, however trivial, has always been collected, processed, filed, and sent to the mother planet. It is hoped that others will join us and the human race will spread further into the solar system. I feel that there must be some kind of back-up storage, so, when asked which area I would like to work in, I chose data inputting and processing, and was assigned to the main office in DN1.

I was curious. I am curious. It is not recommended.

•　　　•　　　•

I was assigned to inputting data, and it is boring. I started by reading everything, claiming I was making sure that it was all correct, but nothing exciting caught my attention and I gradually drifted as I worked. The words and figures became just that — words and figures.

After the Sanderson incident, I find a new focus and begin examining the data I am forwarding. It is boring — still. Everything seems to be fine. In fact, after a few readings, I begin to become uneasy as to how fine everything is. I know we are highly structured and monitored, but surely life cannot be so fine all of the time. Things happen unexpectedly. People are murdered, for goodness sake.

•　　　•　　　•

The reasons we came here are twofold. Our mother planet was struggling under the weight of an increased population. There is not enough room or commodities to go around. We have already colonized Mars and are plundering its resources and have now moved on to the next rock. We are building a new community while we harvest the rich abundance of minerals on and under the icy surface. The supply ship will be here any day now to drop off anything that's been requested and to pick up the ores mined here. The Ceres day is short, the year is long and the temperature cold beyond belief.

"Are we keeping you awake?" My Controller is standing beside me.

"Sorry. I was just thinking," I murmur.

"You have plenty of time to think after work." I am informed. "We cannot afford mistakes."

"I know. I'm sorry." I will have to be more careful.

"Check your work. Make sure it is correct."

"Yes, mam. Straight away, mam." I do check it. It is good. It is too good, but I am saved from further thought by the tone that signifies the end of my working day and the cheery voice saying, "Good-bye, enjoy your evening now." I can think of a reply, but I would be sanctioned if I said it aloud.

HAVE HEARD that some fritillaries are in flower somewhere under one of the domes and decide that I will go and draw them. I love the apposition of the delicate bells in bright gaudy colours growing in the half shade as if shy and retiring. I too can hide in plain sight and think to my heart's content while I am drawing. They are here in DN 1, in the park that is used for recreation and exercise.

DN 1 and DN 2 both have the same layout. They are a kilometer in diameter and have a park in the centre. My dome, DN 2, is basically a dormitory dome where the workers live. We have our own entertainment buildings and gym and sports areas. DN 1 houses the Administrative Centre of the colony, which is huge and takes up a lot of the dome. It even goes deep underground, where the main computer is housed in the cool of the frozen ground. DN 1 also houses the SpaceBus Terminal and an adjacent hotel, although I've never seen anyone use either. Perhaps I'm not there at the right times.

I carry my papers and pencils with me at all times, so there is no issue with going straight to the site. I decide to use the convenience before leaving otherwise I'll be bound to need one as soon as I get settled.

I love the building when everyone has gone. It is so very quiet, and the air is still with just a quiet hum from the ever-working terminals. You can smell the faint aroma they call "fresh air" when there are no other smells to mask it.

The oxygen we breathe in the domes is made on site. Ceres has plenty of water on its surface, most of it frozen. It is gathered, cleaned and used for all our needs: drinking, washing and cooking. A proportion is broken down by electrolysis to create its individual components, hydrogen and oxygen.

All waste is recycled and the resulting products used. The reason we have a series of domes rather than just one big one is so that if something happens in one dome, there will be resources in the others to use to repair the damage and house the personnel until things are back on track. Each dome has its own plant so is able to continue functioning. We are relatively self-sufficient.

•　　•　　•

The convenience doors are the only ones in the whole complex that are not automatic. They are heavy but silent. I pull on the handle when ready to leave, but stop suddenly as I hear voices — my name is mentioned.

I thought I was alone, but there are at least two people here, and they are talking about me. I allow the door to slide so that there is only a slight gap and lean against it in order to hear what is being said.

"She's always had more character than some. There's no real change that I can see." That's my Controller. I recognize her voice. "She should have forgotten everything soon anyway."

"She seems slower than others at forgetting. You know she went to see Enforcement about the Sanderson problem?" This voice is familiar, but I can't put a name to it.

"The Officer reported it correctly. He reckons he managed to fob her off. Don't worry, everyone's different," my Controller continues. "It works more slowly in some than others. She may not be as docile as most but she still follows the rules without question."

"Are you sure?"

"Yes. She should have forgotten everything within three days, five at the latest. I know her and I have no worries. Anyway, we have bigger problems. The SpaceBus is due within the next few days. I'm worried people will notice when it doesn't arrive."

"We'll use the old footage again. It's not like folks'll really remember, is it? You worry too much. The Chief has it all in hand. No-one will notice a thing."

They begin moving down the corridor towards me. I allow the door to shut and slide noiselessly into a cubicle in case my Controller needs to use the convenience. She doesn't. I bustle out, making my presence known, but I needn't have bothered. There is no-one in sight. I have plenty to think about now. And I will need to take much more care.

I hope that I look placid enough on the surface, but underneath my mind is racing. I had heard a lot of information in that short conversation. We rely on the spaceship from the SpaceBus Corp. One should come once a year — an Earth year — with fresh supplies of the things we are short of. Laborers are working hard in domes three through to ten to create farms and manufacturing installations in order that eventually we would become totally self-sufficient, but I doubt they are up and running to full capacity yet due to the "Setback," an accident that happened just under a year ago in one of the Industrial Domes.

Anyway, what about the ores? The ships are supposed to unload the supplies and fill up with carbonates and phyllosillcates to take back to the mother planet. They are reliant on those ores, or so we are told. My head is spinning.

I am finding it difficult to think it all through. Thinking makes me feel muzzy and I get easily confused. What was this about forgetting everything in three days? That needs some serious thinking. I know my memory is bad. I have forgotten old friends and relatives, but I remember my lessons from the education sessions. What's that all about? I can use a technopad to record and analyze and my learnt skills are still intact. Is it because I use them daily?

What I heard answers some questions but poses a whole lot more.

•   •   •

With my mind buzzing as I try to focus, I overlook the fritillaries at first. Eventually I spot them and sit down on the immaculate artificial grass to capture their delicate image. My drawing is a mess. I'm not concentrating. One thing is very clear — I need to make notes. I realized some time ago that if I have no visual reminder, I will forget, eventually. The Controllers are right about that.

I hurriedly scribble an outline of the Data Terminal, a rocket, and a caricature of my Controller before folding the paper tightly and pushing it down into my brassiere. I can't settle, so gather my papers and pencils and try to wander as nonchalantly as possible to the mono-port that will take me back to DN 2 and my apartment.

It is difficult, especially as I meet BJ on my way.

"Hey, Jax."

"Hey yourself."

"Where'yu bin?"

"Drawing fritillaries."

"Huh?"

"Flowers. I've been drawing flowers. In the little park in DN 1."

"Huh. Can I see?" I show him the drawings.

"Huh. You weren't at tea." He's more interested in his belly than my drawings. I've not met anyone else who eats so much.

"I wasn't hungry," I tell him.

"Are you now?"

"Why?"

"I am."

"I thought you'd had your tea?" I query.

"I have but it must be nearly suppertime now." He pulls a pathetic face as if he hadn't eaten all day.

"I don't know where you put it all," I sigh as we turn towards the towers.

We go to eat in the Refectory in his tower because it's the nearest. It doesn't matter where we eat; everything is connected to the main computer and credits deducted accordingly. You just have to key in your Administrative number before the number of the type of meal you want.

I am too anxious to want to eat anything, but select a bowl of the nutritious gloop they serve up as soup and a piece of bread. Food intake is monitored. I have been admonished for not eating enough in my reviews in the past. I tend to rely on the Outlet in my tower. It sells biscuits and cake and other stuff, like chocolate and the cherrysynthe Sanderson loved so much.

"The SpaceBus should be here any day," I say but BJ doesn't comment as he has his mouth full. "What do you think they've done with Sanderson's body?" I ask.

"Who?"

I brush the breadcrumbs from the front of my uniform. "Sanderson. You know, our friend?"

"Never heard of a Sanderson. Are you going to eat that?" He indicates my nearly full bowl, so I push it over to him. It helps if I can take an empty plate to disposal. BJ goes back to eating.

I didn't really need to hear it from the Controllers. People forget. I don't even think about it, as it's so ingrained in daily life. Why? How? I need to get back to my apartment to think, but instead I watch as BJ shovels a glutinous looking pie into his mouth before dragging my bowl towards him and all but inhaling the soup. I am lost in thought and turn what I have learned around and around in my head. By the time he has finished I have got myself into a bit of a state of paranoia, but that leads to an immediate plan of action.

I finally manage to get away from BJ when a work colleague of his arrives and they begin chatting enthusiastically about drains and things. BJ is a plumber and is good at his job, which involves supervising surveys and making reports so that the robots can be programmed to complete a task. I find it boring.

•   •   •

Back in my apartment I spread out some paper and begin my plan. I have decided that if I am using drawing paper the *powers-that-be* will think I am just pursuing my hobby.

I need a code. I can't just write everything down because if it is found I dread to think what might happen. I need to work out a code that will be difficult for anyone to decipher, and that will be a job in itself.

•   •   •

One thousand five hundred hand-picked intelligent people left Earth/Mars for this colony. Everyone had a unique set of skills that would enable them to establish a viable community here. These included astrophysicists, medics, agricultural scientists, eminent geologists, and mechanics of all kinds, all with layers of training. We even had embryonic animals and seeds to stock the farms. These are monitored closely to see how they have developed under the domes on this particular lump of rock, because, even with the best will in the world, there are differences in gravity, rotational pull and lack of lunar influence despite immense scientific intervention.

The community has expanded as was expected. More people arrived from Earth/Mars once we were up and running, and some of us were born here. There are still empty buildings ready for others to come and join us once the results of the experiment show that everything is okay

— if they show that everything is okay. The space ships should be bringing more people to swell this community and relieve the pressure in the Martian colony.

I select a hot drink from the dispenser in my kitchen and activate the television, because if I don't it will be noticed. I don't watch television much and found that it was commented on in my monthly review. They should put something on worth watching. If what the Controllers are saying is true, they could be showing the same old films and documentaries over and over again. No one will notice.

I divide the paper into columns and sit back, thinking about how to head them, when a nasty bout of suspicion sweeps over me. I look at the television screen. Could they be using that to watch what I am doing? Because it is possible, I turn my back to the screen, but the thought has frozen my brain. What would my turned back signal? That I have something to hide?

A sharp knock at the door nearly gives me heart failure. I sit for a moment waiting for its beat to drop to something near normal. There is another tap. If it is anything official, surely the knocking would be more insistent? I relax but only a little.

A rather tall but slightly built girl is standing on the other side of the door when I finally open it. "Oh, hello," she says. "I thought there was someone in. I'm 2:4/2. I live next door."

I am about to say Sanderson lives next door, but manage to shut my mouth in time. I stand back to indicate that she may come in.

Once in, she turns and looks at me. "And you are?"

"Sorry. 5:6/1. But my given name is Jax."

All of the original colonists were given numbers, which were intended to be used for official purposes. My parents were number 0005 and number 0006, and as their first off-spring I was added to their numbers as 5:6/1. It never really took off, although it's still used in certain situations.

"I'm Nan." She smiles at me and then indicates the papers on the table. "Oh, have I disturbed you at work? What are you doing?"

I am about to say, "Nothing" but know that it will sound crass so say instead, "Thinking. I thought if I put my thoughts on paper, then I could make sense of them."

"Not using the techno?"

"No." Anything inputted into the devices can be read by the Controllers. I only use the technopad for things I don't mind them seeing. To Nan I say, "I find this more beneficial to the thought process."

"What are you thinking about? I might be able to help."

What do I say? This Nan is a tad too inquisitive for my liking.

She also seems to need to fill a silence. "I remember you — from the education forums," she says suddenly, as if it has just dawned on her.

That makes me very suspicious.

"You do? Remember me?" I'd finished mandatory education just over a year ago. There is no way that she should be able to recall me, if what I know is true. I don't remember her.

I may never have met her, though. Learning is largely an individual exercise under the domes, although groups are assigned for social interaction based on some unseen formula from above. And then there are the forums of specialist interest, although these are mainly hobbies.

"Yes. You were good at drawing likenesses." She pauses and then whispers, "It got you into trouble."

"You have a good memory."

"It's only been a year or thereabouts. And you did rather stand out. Was it awful? Being dragged to the Big Office? I would have hated it.

"Yes. It was awful and I did hate it," I tell her rather shortly. What is she after?

"What happened to you? In there? We all wanted to know."

I decide that if I am evasive, it will only seem suspect, and goodness knows where it will end. I settle for the truth but do not expand. "I was asked to stop drawing people." *Asked* — if only. "I only draw flowers now. Well, flora. A bit tame, really but people seem to like them."

"Could I see some? Oh, do you think me forward? I do gush on. I've been told about it many times, but I'm interested in everything."

"Have you settled in?" I ask by way of diverting her attention from me.

"Oh, yes. There's nothing much to do is there? Oh, sorry. Am I being a nuisance?"

"No, of course not." But she is. I am concerned that she is a plant. Someone sent to become friendly with me until I forget my paranoia and blurt out something best kept secret. People don't remember things.

"I've got some biscuits," she tells me. "Would you like to join me for tea and snacks? We can get to know each other."

I agree because I am hungry, having not eaten much of the soup earlier, and to do anything else would look suspicious. We go to Nan's apartment, where I try to remain on my guard, but we actually have fun. Nan is intelligent and knowledgeable about any number of things, which makes a change from BJ. We chat over proper tea and the biscuits, which just happen to be chocolate, my favourite. This makes me even more wary.

"How do you know that chocolate biscuits are my favorite?"

"Everyone knows you like chocolate." That's scary.

"Do they?"

"Will you draw my portrait?" The change of subject instantly puts me on alert.

"Sorry. I'm not allowed. I'll draw you a flower though, as a present."

"A present for what?"

"Becoming my friend."

"That's a lovely thought. What will you draw?"

"Wait and see."

I pop back to my room and gather my pencils, pastels, and papers. On my return I draw an anemone and colour it blue to match Nan's eyes. "There. The anemone reminds me of you as well as any portrait."

Suddenly I have my code. I will draw a picture of a flower

to indicate a letter or sound, an anemone for A, begonia for B and so on. Something good has come from our meeting.

By the time I leave, I realize that I like Nan a lot, but I don't trust her. I don't trust her at all.

DESPITE MY INITIAL MISGIVINGS. Nan and I have become friends. I decide it is better to have her close so I can keep an eye on her. We are such good friends that I have nearly forgotten Sanderson. and BJ is becoming more than a little miffed.

"I never see you these days," he mutters over dinner one evening.

"And that's a problem because?" I ask.

"I like you."

BJ is a problem for me. We are destined to be connubial once we reach the age, but I am finding him dull after Nan. We don't have the same interests, not even one. I think Sanderson held us all together. BJ may be good at his work, but I am finding drains a tad mind-numbing. I'm beginning to wonder what criteria the Controllers used when they paired us. I mean, I like BJ, but as to anything else, I really don't feel anything.

We no longer need to be connubial in order for babies to develop. There are ways of getting around having to have sex in order to reproduce. A woman doesn't even need to carry her baby inside her if she doesn't want to. As I said, there are ways. However, after a particularly disturbing incident on Mars in the early days of its colonization, some very in-depth psychological studies took place into human behavior, socialization and the effects of hormones.

I don't recall ever being told what actually happened. It is just known as the "Disturbing Incident."

We may have the technology to do most things using a computer, on our own in our own little cell — sorry — apartment, with robots to do the actual work, but it turns out it's not good for our mental health. This is why we are put to some sort of workplace, in order to feel useful, and why leisure activities are built into the working day. The provision of socialization activities, sport and exercise is considered as important as anything done in the colony.

It is also why we are all paired when we reach the age to leave school, which is eighteen Earth years. We are educated for the work of the dome, and anything else is catered for within our leisure activities. No one questions the way things are done. It's just the way it is.

We are moved to another dome when we become connubial, at the age of twenty-five Earth years. We are expected to sign a declaration with our designated partner that states we will stay together and support each other and do our best to further populate the colony. It's all very business-like. I try not to think about it too much. We have a choice as to whether we want to go to an Industrial or an Agricultural Dome; there are three of each, the same size as Domes 1 and 2, although laid out differently. I've no idea what sort of work we will be expected to do. Robots do the heavy work; we are programmers and scientists. I suppose we'll be trained; there's a lot of that goes on here. I've seen no couples here, nor any children, only workers of roughly my age. I am nineteen Earth years now, nearly twenty.

Nan, unlike BJ, or anyone else for that matter, seems full of life. She enjoys sport and her hobbies include running, swimming and cycling. She says she is a tri-athlete and competes with others on rest days and always wins. The others seem a tad lethargic alongside her. I have taken to going with her to watch. I would like to draw the athletes but know that would bring the wrath of the Controllers down on my head. Besides being active with sports, she likes to explore and pushes the boundaries. One of her games is to go to places we are not allowed and bring back a souvenir to prove that she has done it. I was very wary at first because I thought it a trap.

Not only are our days very structured, but there are places within the domes we are not allowed. Controller-only sites, for instance, or work-related places. There are no cameras monitoring our every move, but alarms will go off if anyone inadvertently enters an area they are not designated to be in. The SET appear out of thin air and the poor miscreant is marched away. Sometimes, in a quiet moment, I wonder how they know. Sometimes I don't want to know.

There are also technosytes on the computer system we are not allowed to visit. A stark warning flashes on the screen should any attempt be made. It's all noted down in our files and "discussed" at our review meetings. By "discussed," I mean you would be subject to a dressing down and temporary loss of privileges. I don't really want to draw attention to myself at this point in time, as I am still considering how to find out what's going on with the SpaceBus. I want to explore, but under the radar, so to speak.

To demonstrate she is willing to take her part in this game, Nan says she has been inside her Controller's bedroom, and brought back a pair of her knickers to prove it. I'm not really convinced, even though the knickers are big enough to belong to the Controller in question.

For my turn, she has suggested that I hack into one of the more general data files in the Protected Data Base; more commonly known as the PDB. I have thought about it. We are allowed to access our own files, although we are not able to alter them. I thought I might try BJ's, as I know his passkey. I'm convinced that as soon as I do, all the alarms in the universe would announce my arrival, the place would go into lock-down, and I would be arrested and deported. I haven't done it. I want to, and not just because Nan told me to. I'm curious but still thinking.

·   ·   ·

I am sitting on the steps of my tower in the never-ending sunshine, a gentle breeze stroking my skin, pondering what to do about it, when along Nan strolls. She is carrying her swimming bag. She does that a lot. She says that the Controllers don't question her if it looks like she is coming or going from her hobby. I can't say much as I usually carry pastels and paper with me. You never know what takes the eye.

"Hey Jax. What's amiss?"

I wonder for a minute if she knows what I'm thinking. Do the Controllers know? Does anyone know? Is it all being kept quiet so that I find enough rope to hang myself?

"Just thinking," I tell her.

"You do a lot of that. It's not healthy. Not in this sunshine."

"The sun's always shining. There's no point waiting for it to go in so I can think," I snarl. An underground watering system negates the need for rain in the areas where real plants are grown.

"Is it that time of the month?"

"What's it to you if it is?"

"You're a bit snappy, is all. Come on, let's do something exciting." I don't answer so she continues. "If you won't hack the PDB let's try and get to the Agricultural Domes."

"That's *above* our designation," I remind her.

"Phuddle. If we did what we were allowed to do, it wouldn't be fun. You are in one today. I'll go on my own if that's the way you feel." When I don't answer she quips, "There's bound to be some different species of flora there."

"Okay. I'll go with you," I sigh. "We can pick some of the flowers as our souvenir." It will keep her off my back while I think about the PDB. I suppose it will be interesting to see the other domes.

The Agricultural Domes are separated from ours by a long interconnecting tunnel. It runs for ten kilometers, roughly following the cave system through a mountain range where it is impossible to build. I've never been. No one I know has ever been. I've not thought about it before. We've been told it's above our designation and have just accepted it. We have been told that we will be taken to both the Agricultural and the Industrial domes in our connubial pairs so we can see what's what before we have to make our choice. Nan is opening my eyes to the amount of control we live with here.

"How are we going to get to the Agricultural Domes? Have you thought about that?" I am a tad narky today.

Only the 'bots and maintenance staff go outside of the domes due to the intense cold and incredibly thin atmosphere, and humans have to wear highly protective clothing, so a rail system was built through the tunnels to make it easier to travel from one dome to another. Mono-pods run through the tunnels, but our reasons for using them are always checked, and as we don't have a valid one, we would be stopped and sent back. Getting a suit is outside our designation as well. Also, there is the possibility that whatever killed Sanderson is lurking among the ice and rocks, but that's my theory. No-one else can remember him.

"We'll go through the inspection channels," Nan tells me matter-of-factly.

Trust Nan to know about them. Perhaps I'm too paranoid. I suppose we should all realize that there must be inspection routes in case of power failure. It's a given, really. As is the fact that we are all tracked all of the time. I am not paranoid enough.

"We both have a work-break tomorrow," she reminds me. "We'll go then. If we set off really early, we'll have all day to get there and back before tea."

I never give a thought to our presence in the dome being missed.

•   •   •

Come the morning, we set off idling our way towards the nearest mono-port as if on a day out taking in the views. I carry my folio and pastels in a carrier on my back and Nan has a rucksack with sandwiches and drinks for lunch. A number of our data processors like to sit and watch the mono-pods when not at work. It's one of the prices they pay for being far too clever for their own brains. We mingle quietly. Data processors are not known for their sociability and so we glide gradually and largely unnoticed over to the PRIVATE KEEP OUT sign printed in red and intended to be scary on a barely concealed door.

It's not locked and I just presume that it's kept unlocked during the day for easy access, even though every other door in the place needs a code or fingerprint in order to open them. Besides, who in their right mind would want to walk through inspection tunnels unless they had to?

The tunnel is dimly lit by emergency lighting and just a bit grimy, as if what is not seen doesn't matter. We can hear nothing untoward inside so creep ahead, ears straining to catch any sounds that might indicate the possibility of being caught.

We trudge on for what feels like forever, the way seeming long as journeys do when you have no real idea of the length. We dare not speak normally, so use signs and whispers when we need a rest.

"What time do you think it is?" I whisper eventually.

"Not sure. It must be midday. I feel hungry enough for it to be lunchtime," Nan returns.

That's the trouble with everything being so regulated and dished up to you on a plate; you lose a lot of skills. I have lost the power to estimate most things. I agree with her because

I am hungry too, but we have been physically active. Normally, we are sat at terminals. Nan insists we stop, so we do, and sit on our rucksacks to eat our lunches and drink our fruit juice before ploughing on.

It is not long after that Nan suddenly stops in front of me. "Can you smell that?"

I have been smelling it for a few minutes, but it is now strong enough for me to cover my nose. "What is it? It's foul."

"Fermented waste."

"It doesn't smell like waste."

"And you know what fermented waste smells like?"

In our sanitized world, I have not had the opportunity to smell anything that unpleasant. "And you do?" I snap.

She doesn't answer my question but suggests, "We must be nearly there."

"It's taken longer than you said," I pout. "Will we be back in time for tea?"

"Late sitting, I should think." Nan doesn't appear concerned. "Come on."

We creep around the bend and into the glow of sunlight. The door at the end of the tunnel stands open and we edge through. I expect to be in an Agricultural Dome mono-port.

I bang into Nan's back. "Move, Nan." She doesn't. I push around the side of her and see why she has stopped.

There is no port. The tracks just peter out into a mountain of blocks, which look as if they have fallen in an untidy heap from wherever they should have been. There is a dome, fortunately for us, but the air, although breathable, smells foul. There is no sign of life, flora or fauna; just lumps of decaying buildings. It's bitterly cold. There is no heating and no artificial light here. The glow we can see comes from the real sun, hundreds of millions of miles away, shining through the transparent dome.

I pull at Nan's overalls. "Come on. Let's get out of here."

I can hardly bear to think what this means. I decide that if I can't see it, it doesn't exist. I can pretend all is well. The Controllers wouldn't allow any harm to come to us, surely.

"Nan. Please. I don't like this. Come on." I turn as if to leave.

Nan steps further into the dome and, involuntarily I turn back and start to follow. I don't feel I can leave her however daft she's being.

"Please."

Something is so very wrong. I take a breath. Silly me. There are other domes. The others will be fine. It's just this one. This must be the one that was damaged in the "Setback." Our food has to come from somewhere.

"We need a souvenir," Nan whispers.

"For goodness sake. There's nothing to take. Let's just get out of here."

"Of course there is," Nan turns to me, grinning.

I do not recognize the face I am seeing. I step back in fear. What have I done?

Nan's face settles back into the one I am familiar with. "It's okay. It's safe enough at the moment. This way." She runs off over the blackened ground.

I decide there is no way I'm going with Nan. It's up to her if she wants to run about in this blackened desolation. I'm scared and cold and tired and decide she's made her choice, and it won't be my fault if anything happens to her. I turn back to the door, but it has shut behind us. I hadn't noticed that. There is no handle. I search the door and the surrounding wall for a keypad or screening device, but there is nothing. I panic and rub my hands all over before beating my fists against the door. There is no response.

"Here." I nearly jump out of my skin. Nan is back, holding a coat. "I told you there was something here."

The coat is an old uniform cold weather issue. It is torn and dirty, stained with something I will not give thought to. "Put it on. You'll freeze without it," warns Nan. I'm shaking with cold and can only do as she says.

"Who are you?" I whisper between chattering teeth.

"I'm Nan. This way."

"No — really. Who are you? Are you working for the Controllers?" I am aware my voice sounds panicky.

She laughs. "Is that what you think?"

"I do. I think you are trying to trap me into doing something they can sanction me for."

"Why on Ceres would I do that?"

"Because I don't forget."

"Couldn't be further from the truth. Come on before we freeze. We need to keep moving."

"How will we get back?" I indicate the closed door. "The door's shut and won't open."

"That's okay, I know the code," she says with a smile, and hurries off further into the damaged dome.

Because I am so cold, I follow her, and only gradually become aware that she isn't wearing a coat and she doesn't seem all that bothered by the freezing air. We lope on at an easy pace, giving me time to think. My mind makes up all sorts of scenarios and not one of them has me coming out of this in one piece.

"Will you hurry up?" Nan grabs my arm in a painful grip, her fingers digging into my flesh like claws through the thick coat.

I almost drop to the ground as a ripple passes over her face. A thin tongue glides across her lips and a frisson of lightning sparks in her eyes. I look back, but she is just Nan, with her just-Nan hand on my forearm.

I shake my arm to loosen her grip. "Who are you?"

"Not the time. I'll tell you when we're safe. They're bound to be on to us by now. I am a friend, that will do for now. Come on."

I follow because I don't know what else to do. All I can think is that I was right to be wary of her, followed closely by how do I get out of this?

It's only one kilometre across the dome, but it seems a long way when you're tired, cold, and frightened. Eventually, we reach the end and Nan leads the way into the adjoining tunnel. This tunnel is not as long as the first and soon opens into the next dome.

I have no idea where we are. I was hoping to see fertile fields and sleek cattle, or perhaps Industrial buildings all working away, but the vista is even more blighted than the last. It looks as if a bomb has dropped and razed everything into an even plateau of ash. The dome has obviously been damaged and botched repairs are in place.

We stop for breath. The air is thin and tastes disgusting.

"Is this where it happened?" I ask. Nan nods.

"I believe so. We know it was in an Industrial Dome. Either this one or the next one to it."

"Are they ...? Are they all the same do you think?"

"The Industrial Domes? Yes."

"How do you know all this, Nan?" I want to know. There are too many unanswered questions surrounding her, and I am becoming more and more afraid.

"I'll tell you everything when we're safe. I told you."

I sit with a thump on the hard ground. Little clouds of ash swirl up and then settle around me. "The ships have stopped coming." Nan nods as if it is no surprise. "We keep forgetting." She doesn't respond. "I said, we ..."

"I know."

"What about the Agricultural Domes? Are they alright?" Nan gives me a strange look. "God, Nan. What's going to happen to us?"

She doesn't answer, just grabs my wrist, and pulls me up. "We can't stay here. It's dangerous. Come on."

"How dangerous? Radiation?"

"That as well."

I pull back. It's just one shock after another. "As well as what?"

"The Beasts are loose," she says as she races off over the desolation.

At the mention of "Beasts" I see, with startling clarity, a vision of Sanderson as I found him. He is sprawled at an impossible angle with large furrows of flesh gouged from his torso. I can smell the blood and the contents of his insides as if I am standing beside him. I see the flick of his cowlick so vividly that I almost reach out to brush it out of his eyes. Blue, open eyes that stare at me pleading for my help. It is a memory so strong that I stumble and try to shake it from my head. I have never, to my knowledge, had a recollection so strong or so detailed since the incident in my Lead Educator's office.

"What Beasts?" I ask. Nan is too far ahead to hear my feeble gasp. "What Beasts?" I yell.

Nan stops and looks back at me shaking her head. She waits for me to catch up.

Did we bring Beasts? I try to remember. It was before my time but I'm sure we would have learnt in school if we had Beasts in the Agricultural Domes. We had been told about the domestic animals and the detailed research into their growth and well-being. But then I could have forgotten.

Nan puts her finger to her lips. "Don't advertise our presence," she whispers.

"What Beasts?" I whisper back.

"I'll tell all when we are safe." Nan promises. "They got in during the "Setback."."

""Setback?" It's a bloody disaster." I don't usually swear like that; it is forbidden in the domes, but I am so scared.

"We've got to keep moving. This dome is not safe. Save your breath." We set off at a jog.

We are encouraged to keep fit and I attend the gym attached to my tower for my allotted time. I am glad that I do now, as the pace Nan sets is pretty testing, and I am still clutching my artist's bag. We reach the tunnel at the opposite end of the dome much more quickly than I expect. Nan stops by the opening and waits for me. The short Ceres day is beginning to reach its end and the dome is darkening rapidly. I follow. I am tiring by this time, although Nan seems unfazed by it all. The door to the tunnel is closed but Nan opens it easily enough.

"This tunnel is a bit longer," Nan whispers as we creep through. "Please, Jax. Just follow my lead. It's for your own safety."

I nod but have no idea what she's talking about. I've gone beyond scared or surprised. I'm just befuddled with shock.

There is no light in the tunnel; the blackness solid enough to touch. I fumble with my technopad, but Nan puts her hand over it.

"Don't. It's not safe," she whispers, even though there is no one to hear us. "They can track us through its signal. Hold my belt and follow me." She undoes her belt and puts one end in my hand and closes my fingers over it as if reassuring me that everything will be fine.

I don't like the blackness; it makes me feel claustrophobic. But what choice do I have?

Nan's idea of longer is so right, but we trudge on and eventually I see light ahead through the clear window in a closed door. It's got to be electricity, as the planet's day will be at an end and the sun will have set beyond the horizon. I begin to feel more optimistic as we emerge into the artificial daylight.

We are in the patched-up remains of a mono-port. I can see three or four towers like the ones in Domes 1 and 2, and pavements between. It all looks innocuous and normal, if a little untidy compared to my dome. The towers have been made good, the blocks a slightly different shade where they have been repaired. The buzz from the power generators in the domes I work and live in is ever there, but it is muted to a vibration felt only in moments of extreme quietness and inactivity. The rumble here is invasive, albeit at a low level.

I turn to Nan, but then decide I shall add it to the list of questions I intend to ask when it is safe to do so. It is warm and light, and at the moment that is all I ask. We can talk about the trouble we're in later. Being sent back to the home planet feels more like a reward than a punishment after what I've seen.

AS WE LEAVE the mono-port, a tall man steps out in front of Nan. No, not a tall man — a *stretched* man. That's the immediate impression I get; a man who has been stretched until he is very tall.

He bends from the waist and Nan tells him something in a dialect I can't understand. The stretched man uncoils and looks at me long and hard, and then inclines his head and smiles a toothless smile as he holds out a hand. I wonder if I'm expected to shake it like I've seen people do in the endless old films the Controllers keep putting on the television, but Nan fumbles for her technopad and gives it to him before turning to me.

"Give him your TP." She sees my hesitation and says testily. "I told you the Controllers can track you through it. Attercliffe will sort it." I hurriedly pass the TP to the stretched man before it bites me, and he points into the dome. Nan turns to me and encourages me on, grabbing my wrist. "Attercliffe won't hurt you as long as you toe the line. This way. You need to be introduced so that everyone knows you."

"What will he do if I don't? Toe the line?" I shudder, but Nan just grins. "You planned this from the start," I gasp.

"We'll explain everything once you've been introduced."

"Introduced to whom?"

"The Caputa." Nan pushes her way into the nearest tower. "You have to be approved by The Caputa before you can go anywhere or meet anyone in this dome."

"Why?"

"It's dangerous out there. We need to know we can trust you."

"And The Caputa will do that?" I look askance at Nan. I have nothing that can corroborate who I am and my intentions. "How?"

"She has her ways. Now come on. This way. We need to shower and change. The domes may be contaminated with heaven knows what. We can't take the chance."

The tower is set out in the same way as the ones in DN 2 and we head for the gym, which seems quite small to me compared with my own. We are obviously expected to use its showering facilities, which are utilitarian and immaculate. There are piles of towels and two sets of clean overalls and underwear on the bench outside of the shower cubicles and two pairs of soft shoes underneath.

"Just pile your dirty stuff in the bin by the door. Someone will burn it later," Nan instructs.

The soap is coarse and smells faintly of herbs. There is no shampoo, so I use the soap on my hair. I welcome the shower and would have stayed under the warm water for longer, but Nan is impatient to be out. As soon as we are ready, she leads the way further into the building. I begin to follow but stop suddenly as, in front of Nan, is the most grotesque little man I have ever seen. She rushes straight up to him and speaks again in the clipped language I heard her speak earlier. She reaches back and grabs my wrist pulling me forward.

"The Caputa?" I whisper.

"Oh no. This is the guard. You can't get to see The Caputa without his permission."

The guard looks me up and down. I return the compliment. He is squat and very bloated with not a single hair anywhere in sight. Instead, all the skin I can see, which is a fair bit, is completely tattooed with pictures of animals the like of which I have never seen, not even on my technopad. I start to shiver under his scrutiny when he clicks his fingers and a small, pale boy emerges from behind the Admin counter. The guard whispers something in his ear. The boy stares at me and then runs in the direction of the lifts.

I don't hear the whine of the elevator, but it is not long before the child is back. He nods to the guard and beckons to us.

"We use the stairs," Nan tells me. "Power is not wasted where it is not needed." I open my mouth to ask how she knows, but snap it shut again. I know, I will find out when it's safe.

We continue up to the top floor, which I find has been knocked about a bit — a lot, really. Most of it has been turned into one open-plan apartment. It is well furnished, not sumptuous but utilitarian and comfortable. I see no-one. Nan makes me stand just inside the threshold. We wait.

Eventually I hear a rustle and, without my seeing movement, someone is standing at the back of the room. This person is tall, stretched, and slim to the point of thinness, making the head appear to be overly large above the shoulders. I realize that it is a woman as she moves nearer. She is beguiling in a strange sort of way. Her skin is naturally pale but there is a healthy glow about her. Her hair is long and shines with all the colours of leaves in our simulated autumn, shades of green among the golds and reds, and is bound in many braids over her shoulders and down her back. She is dressed in a loose robe of some sort of woven fabric. The colours of the robe match the colours in her hair and seem to swirl into each other as she moves, making my head spin.

But it is her eyes that scare me the most. They are huge, clear and vividly blue. She stares at me without blinking. She is so still I begin to wonder if she is an automaton that I failed to notice when we first arrived.

"So, we have another one?" The voice is deep and startling in its suddenness. I think I expected her to speak in that strange language Nan has been using, but she speaks perfect English, the common language of the known universe.

"Yes, Caputa. This is Jax." Nan introduces me.

"Jax?"

"Jac … I'm sorry." I clear my throat. "Jacqueline LeBrun." I never use my full name. No-one ever uses my full name unless I'm in trouble, but I feel compelled to say it now.

"Much nicer than Jax. Jax is so hard." She has stepped forward and it takes all my willpower not to step back. "So, you remember?"

I cast a glance at Nan. How does she know? I nod, not trusting myself to speak.

A long slender arm emerges from the robe and a finger beckons me forward. I take the step. Another arm snakes from the cloak and the hand spans the top of my head, clamping down and massaging my skull. A not unpleasant feeling, even though I want to step away from it.

"You remember everything?" Yet another arm coils from the cloth and strokes the outer contours of my body, making me feel uncomfortable. It's like she's frisking me.

"No." I try to shake my head, but her fingers prevent it from moving. "I remember some things, but I have to work at it — leave myself clues." She looks deeply into me. I don't mean through my eyes as most people do, but I feel her inside my head as if searching my memories. "I'm remembering more since I left the dome — my dome." I am feeling dizzy and ever so slightly unwell.

"Do you remember the "Setback"?"

"Only what we've been told. It seems to be the excuse for everything."

The woman smiles, "I like this one. She'll be very useful."

How does she know? She's only just met me. What has she found buried in my sub-conscious that would make me useful? As what?

I try to step back, but her fingers seem stuck to my head.

"Don't be afraid. We will not harm you. I suppose you have questions." She releases her grip on my head and I nod, but as I do so her fingers slip to my neck and her nails gouge a furrow. I squeal, as much from the suddenness of it as the pain it causes. She releases me and shows me something, tiny like the tip of a calligraphy pen.

"What is that?" I ask as I feel the back of my neck. She passes me a soft pad with another hand, and I dab it to the spot, soaking up the blood from the wound she has given me.

"Something you should be grateful to lose. This little chip tells the computers in Domes 1 and 2 everything there is to know about you. We've never tested how far that range is, but we don't think it comes this far." She shatters it between her fingers. "It's best to get rid. Now you'll eat. You can ask your questions over the meal. If you like the answers we'll move on from there. Agreed?"

I nod. I have no other choice.

"You may tell everyone that I approve, Nan."

We are obviously dismissed, and Nan leads me back down two flights of stairs to the ground floor. "We eat here." Nan explains.

"How many arms has that woman got?" I want to know.

"You mean The Caputa? Six, but just the two legs."

"Like Kali?"

Nan just shrugs and leads me out. Religion is not so big on Ceres. I know about Kali through my art sessions. Nan has no reason to know who I'm talking about.

I thought I would feel more able to cope once clean and appropriately dressed, but shock is setting in. I am cold and cannot stop shaking. The back of my neck is stinging now, although I think the bleeding has stopped.

"You need some sugar," says Nan, looking at me sideways. She takes me along the corridor and into the communal eating room.

The man she called Attercliffe is there at a table set for half a dozen people. It is one of a number of tables in the room.

Nan throws herself down in the chair next to the stretched man. "This is Jax," she tells him in English as I take the seat beside her. He nods in my direction. "The Caputa has approved." He nods again.

A rattling attracts our attention and I turn to see a plump, comfortable-looking woman loping over carrying a tray laden with mugs and jugs.

"Ah, tea." Nan jumps up and helps the woman with the tray. "Janet, this is Jax. The Caputa approves." Janet nods. "Jax — Janet."

Janet nods again in my direction and then disappears back the way she came. Do these people not speak?

"I'll pour." Nan sets about pouring tea and passing the mugs round. "Sugar for you, Jax, whether you like it or not."

"I'd rather have chocolate." I hate the thought of sugar in my tea.

"Not here, I'm afraid. We don't run to chocolate. Ah, here's Janet back with the food." She jumps up again. My head is spinning with her. She's so full of life.

The smell of the food precedes the dish, and it is heavenly. Nan clears a space on the table and Janet lays down a tray of warm, crisp pastries dripping with different coloured syrups. I realize how hungry I am. It seems forever since we left our dome.

"It's only leftovers from breakfast but I thought your friend looked as if she needed sugar," observes Janet.

Only leftovers? It's a banquet compared with what we are served for breakfast — or any other meal, come to that. The tea has a scented light taste the like of which I have never known before. The pastry is sweet, crisp and light, melting in my mouth, and the syrups are tangy and fruity. It is then that what she has said registers in my overloaded brain.

"Breakfast? What time is it?" I look around for the ever-present clock, but there isn't one in this Refectory.

"Middle of the morning. Just after ten." Janet doesn't hesitate.

"But we left our dome hours ago. It must be later than that."

"We might not be synched with your domes," Janet informs me. "We set our own times when we re-programmed the computers."

"The "Setback"?" I ask, and Janet nods. "What happened?" All three silently turn to look at me at the same time. The effect is scary, and I involuntarily sit back.

"There was an explosion." The deep voice comes from behind; warm, making my spine tingle with anticipation. No-one looks up.

The owner of the voice moves around me and sits in the seat next to mine. Open-faced with dark, sparkling eyes full of intelligence; he looks at me as if no-one else matters. I am besotted.

"Noah." He introduces himself. "And you must be Jax. The Caputa has approved I have been given to understand."

I put out my hand to take his proffered one only to find I'm still holding the bloody pad. I quickly stuff it in my pocket, hoping he hasn't noticed, and take his, which is warm and dry. I could hold it forever but feel myself blushing even more and I let go, tucking my hands under the table.

"So, you want to know what happened." He carries on without waiting for my answer. "We think there was an explosion in one of the Industrial Domes." He pauses as if thinking about how to continue. "As you must know the domes of the colony, together with the corridors and mono-links that join them, form a shape almost like a helix due to the lie of the land. Those domes nearest were devastated by the blast. We took some damage, as you may have noticed, but the hilly land between saved us from devastation. The two Admin Domes, which are furthest away, hardly felt anything. The tunnels are longer from the Admin Domes to the Agricultural and Industrial

Domes, and run through very hilly ground. That shielded you from the worst."

"How many domes are left?" I don't trust that any were, apart from DN 1, my own, and this one.

"Domes 1 and 2 are working as normal," chips in Nan. "That's why you think everything's alright."

"Hardly," mutters Janet. I turn to look at her, but she turns away under Noah's stare.

"It's not Jax's fault. It happened when she was a child." He speaks softly to her despite the glare.

I am stunned. "What do you mean? It happened last year." I turn to each, but no-one says anything. "Didn't it?" I look at Noah.

"It happened fourteen Earth years ago or thereabouts."

"But ..."

"I know what you're told. And I know about the forgetfulness. The drug they put in the air in order to keep the peace. It cannot last."

"I know. There's been no SpaceBus for a couple of years."

"Fourteen," snaps Janet. "They think we're all dead. And how can we tell them otherwise, with what's going on?" She scowls at Noah.

"Janet, this tea's cold. I'm sure Noah would like some fresh. I know I would." Nan jumps up and starts to gather the crockery. "Come, I'll give you a hand."

Noah waits until Janet and Nan have left for the kitchen before turning back to me. "You mustn't mind Janet. She lost her whole family in what you call the "Setback." She was on an educational trip to the Agricultural Domes when it happened. It was fortunate that most of the children were. Those in the Industrial Domes never stood a chance.'

"So, what happened? I thought we transferred to the Industrial or Agricultural Domes when we became connubial."

"That wasn't what happened before the "Setback." We were assigned to a dome according to our skill set."

I struggle to get my head around this concept. We are told that at the age of twenty-five we are transferred to a dome of our choice. But there are no domes. Noah is speaking and I lose my train of thought.

"We don't really know what happened for sure. It could have been an explosion from within or an attack from without. We lost contact with the rest of the colony, and we had our own problems. The domes had cracked and needed mending before we lost everything. Some of the buildings were damaged, people killed and injured. By the time we had sorted the most immediate of these issues and cleared the tunnels, we found the doors to the other domes closed to us."

"But we came through. How come you don't make your presence known to the Controllers?'

"Eventually we were able to open up the passageways, but the first people through were killed on sight."

I am incredulous. "Why would anyone do that?"

"Contamination. At the time, we all had to consider the possibility of radiation poisoning. Although measurements are a little high, it's largely unfounded. Chemicals were used to separate the ores, and so pollution from that was — and still is — a consideration. Both are measured on a daily basis. But, of course, the Beasts were loose."

"Nan mentioned the Beasts. What Beasts are these?"

"Did I hear my name?" Nan is coming out of the kitchen. She places a tray on the table. "Jan sends her apologies, but she has some chores to finish."

"Is she alright?" Noah asks.

"Yes. She's a werrit. If everything was fine, she'd worry there was nothing to worry about."

"She lost everything," says Noah quietly.

"She wasn't the only one. Some of us deal with it." Nan busies herself with pouring the tea.

I have a number of questions I want to ask, but a voice breaks into the conversation. "Is that tea being poured?" The voice again comes from behind me, and I half turn to see an attractive woman heading for the table.

Noah gets up, "Braithe." He takes her hand and kisses her cheek taking a little longer than a normal greeting. "Come, meet Jax. The Caputa has approved."

Braithe isn't just attractive. She's eye catching in an unconventional sort of way. She's tall, almost as tall as Noah, but not stretched like some of those I've met. Her skin makes me think of the synthetic cream we get on high days, and her hair is a deep auburn, curling down her back in thick heavy waves. She has big green eyes which have hardly left the man beside her. She's full of life and colour. Altogether she's very unforgettable.

She finally tears herself from Noah. "Hello. I'm Braithe, Noah's connubie."

Phuddle. I might have known. He's much older than me anyway. I take the offered hand and shake it politely.

"You must tell me all about yourself." She struggles out of her heavy coat and sits beside Noah. Even the shapeless bags we are all wearing look good on her.

I tell my story, as limited as it is, because I don't remember much of my early life at all. I suddenly have the thought that I may have no family either and my throat closes. I wave the kind concerns away, but everything comes together to undo me, and I burst into tears. I am mortified. I am grieving. I am scared.

●　　●　　●

"I thought you were stronger than that?" Nan pouts as soon as we reach her room. It seems I'm to share with her until a place can be found for me.

"I'm sorry. I don't know what came over me," I mutter.

"I rescued you because I thought you would help us."

"I will. I just need a bit of time to come to terms with all this. Didn't it come as a shock to you?" I am cross with her. We all tackle adversity differently. Some of us are stronger and more able to cope than others.

"I've lived it all my life. Well, nearly."

"You? How? What?" I'm confused. "You said you remembered me from school."

"That was a lie. To see what you were made of. I got it from Sanderson."

"Sanderson? You knew Sanderson?"

"He was my brother. My half-brother, really. His mum had an affair with my dad." She looks at me and hurriedly carries on. "I didn't ask for details."

"Well, you wouldn't, I suppose. Not of your dad."

She hesitates. Then, "My dad isn't from Earth. Not strictly what you would call human." I think my brain will explode if I hear much more. I wait for her to explain.

She swallows and then dives in. "He's an Agamidonid. From Agamidonae. It's a planet in the constellation you call Cepheus. The eastern arm between Gamma Cephei and the Pole star."

I find my mouth won't work.

"Say something."

I shake my head.

"You don't think you're the only inhabitants of the universe, surely?"

I shake my head again.

"You're so up yourselves, you humans. You think you're so clever. The Caputa is an Arak. The Araks conquered space distance centuries ago. They go all over the place. Your Kali was one of them." She's getting very excited.

I close my eyes. My brain is overloaded, and I just want to sleep.

"I'm sorry," I say because I don't know what else to say. "Can this wait? You can blame me for all the troubles humankind has wrought tomorrow but now I just need to sleep."

Nan opens her mouth, but I am saved from her next tirade by a knock at the door. Braithe pops her head round without waiting to be invited. "Hi girls. I've found a room for Jax if she'd like to come with me. It'll save you squashing up in here."

"Whatever," Nan waves her arms and turns away.

I drag myself from her chair and stumble towards Braithe.

"Get some rest Nan. You've done a good job. It can't have been easy." She signals me through the door, which she closes gently behind her. She takes my hand and leads me away from Nan's room.

"I thought you might like somewhere quiet while you think through what you've seen and heard today. Nan can be a bit tense after an assignment. She puts her all into her character."

"Thank you," I whisper.

She stops a couple of doors down from Nan's and ushers me into the room. It is like the one I have in DN 2. Even the colours are the same.

"I'm confused," I tell her. "We were told that everything was alright after the "Setback." That you were all working hard to put it right. And then I see ..." I pause.

"Well, we are working hard to put things right. We need to survive. Look, you're all in. I've made sure there's tea and biscuits in your cupboards. You can have a snack. Take another shower; go to bed if you need to. Sort out the time difference and we'll talk tomorrow."

I don't bother with any tea, or a shower. I just fall into bed, where I dream of BJ and wake with tears on my cheeks. What have I come to?

MY BODY CLOCK is all to pot so I've no idea what the time is when I wake up. I used to be ready to put a chair through the ridiculous clock in our domes, but just now I would relish the normality of its chirpily annoying voice. I am wide awake so take a long hot shower and put on the clothes they gave me yesterday as I have nothing else.

Then, because I don't know what else to do I make my way to the Refectory to see if anyone is about. There would always be someone on duty in DN 1 and 2 regardless of the hour. The artificial sun is up so I decide that it can't be that early. I must have slept for hours.

There is a delicious smell of baking bread and my tummy rumbles in anticipation. Attercliffe is leaving the Refectory as I enter and nods as he walks by. Noah is sitting in the same place as I left him the day before. He is poring over some papers on the table. He has a writing implement in his hand and is making notes. I stand and watch quietly for a moment wondering if he has moved at all, when Janet spots me from the kitchen.

"Come in. Come in. We don't bite." She scuttles over with a plate of warm pastries and a jug of syrup. Her round face is red and shiny from the heat of the kitchen and a few fair wisps of hair curl from the confines of the scarf wrapped around her head. "I'll bring the tea."

Noah moves some of the papers so that I can set myself a place. He nods a greeting and then gets back to whatever it is he's doing. I'm too nervous to sit next to him, so take a seat as far away as I can. I find I'm now sitting directly opposite, which I feel is worse, but Janet appears and puts a pot and a mug in front of me, so moving would seem rude.

"There you are. I can't stop and chat. I've breakfasts to get ready. You are an early bird."

I look up and smile, but she's already gone, and I feel an idiot grinning into space, so I turn it on Noah, but he looks far too busy to chat. I turn my attention to my food.

The pastry cracks loudly in the silence as I break into it, splaying crumbs across the table. I hastily sweep them up and drop them onto my plate. I try and chew quietly, but every crunch seems to echo. I pick up the pot to pour the tea but as I try to ask Noah if he wants some, a crumb becomes lodged in my throat, and I end up coughing and spraying him with saliva coated pastry flakes. He moves the papers further away. Why isn't he using a technopad? You can wipe a technopad.

I can't seem to dislodge the crumb and have just reached the conclusion that I am about to die when Braithe and Nan wander in. Nan gives me a hearty thwack on the back, and I feel the pastry move. She pours me a mug of tea and sits beside me.

"Sip that. It'll ease the throat. She rubs my back for a few minutes, until she's satisfied I'm okay.

"Are you alright?" Braithe looks at me while sitting next to Noah, her hand on his.

I nod, tears streaming down my face, eyes bulging and spittle dripping from my chin. I drag my sleeve across my face leaving a trail of slime.

"Th… th… thanks," I stutter. "A crumb went the wrong way."

"Didn't you see her choking?" Braithe admonishes Noah.

"You arrived before I could do anything," he tells her without conviction.

She shakes her head and turns to me. "How are you this morning? Choking apart? Feel up to a look around? See how we work? It will help you to make up your mind."

"Make up my mind about what?" I ask as I wipe my face. In front of Noah of all people!

"Whether you like us enough to stay and help us."

"I thought I was staying."

"You can stay if you want to. Nobody's going to force you to do anything you don't want," she tells me, before pausing as if thinking. "Unless it creates danger for the rest of us."

"What will happen if I go back now?"

"Nothing. They forget things in your dome. They'll forget you were missing. You'll forget us in time. We rely on it," Nan reminds me.

"I don't think the Controllers forget much," I tell her as I think back to the conversation I overheard when I was in the lavatory. "In fact, I don't think they forget at all."

Noah's head swings round. He might not have heard me choking but he heard that. "Why would you say that?" he asks a look of concern on his face.

I explain about the two I heard talking. "I can't be sure. It was just an impression I got from the conversation."

"We thought they put a drug in the air," Braithe muses.

"If they did that everyone would be affected, surely," I suggest.

"It could be in the food," Nan observes. "Or a residue from the 'Setback'."

"Whatever it is, it's in our interest to know who is and is not affected." Noah is obviously worried. "It puts our people at risk."

"You must have known that already," I tell him. "You knew I remembered things. Isn't that why you sent Nan to me?"

"No. We didn't know that you don't forget as easily as some. Not until we met you. We just knew that you had been reported by the SEO in DN 2."

"How do you know about that?"

"We have our means." Nan turns to me. "You were asking after Sanderson. You must have remembered him to ask after him."

"What I don't understand is how I can remember my lessons and things that are important to day-to-day tasks, but why not people and some events?"

"Oh that's easy," Nan tells me. "They use subliminal learning when you're asleep. It used to annoy the crap out of me when I was trying to drop off."

"How come I never sussed it?" I ask.

"You must be a heavy sleeper," Nan shrugs. "Also the drug doesn't seem to have the same effect on those of us who aren't totally human. My DNA is mixed, as is that of all our operatives who go into the Admin Domes."

That made a lot of sense but my brain is spinning; there's so much going on I had no idea about. My memory is still poor and I wonder how long it will take to right itself. Will it ever be right?

"What are you planning?" I ask.

"Planning?" Nan stares at me.

"Yes. What are you planning? In the Admin Domes? You are obviously planning something. You haven't brought me here for my scintillating company," I quip. "So, are you going to tell me what you're planning before I decide what to do?"

Noah puts down his writing implement and looks straight at me. "No.'

For some reason his tone puts my back up. "I need to know what's going on before I make up my mind. The Caputa approves, I believe you say."

"Indeed, The Caputa approves, but that does not mean we are going to let you into all our secrets before *I* approve. The Caputa does not put herself in the dangers that we do." There's a sharp, collective intake of breath. It appears knocking The Caputa is frowned on, but Noah carries on regardless. "We guard The Caputa. Our lives are put at risk on a daily basis. By all means go and look around. Ask any question you like, and it will be answered. From the information you glean, you can make up your mind. If you agree to stay with us, you will be given all the information you need to know.

"Need to know?"

"Need to know." Very final. He carries on. "You will be told everything you need to know and nothing more. That way no one person can betray another."

"Is anyone likely to do that?"

"You never can tell. It depends on what they do to you." He goes back to his papers. This interview has obviously finished. Not that I want to find out the sort of things *they* might do to a person anyway.

There is silence around the table for a few more seconds before Braithe smiles sweetly at me and Nan. "Nan. Perhaps you'd like to show Jax around. Take a break before your next assignment." Nan looks at her as if she's spoken in a foreign language. "As soon as you like." We have been dismissed.

•   •   •

Nan doesn't speak until we are well away from the building. Then she sort of huffs before deciding what to say. "I'm sorry about last night. The way I acted." Nan doesn't look at me as she speaks. She's much calmer today. I can feel it in the way she speaks and moves.

"That's alright," I reassure her.

She clears her throat. "I get a bit wound up over assignments and then ..."

"It's okay. Really. Braithe explained how difficult things can be."

"Friends again?"

"Friends again."

We had been walking in silence but now that Nan has broken it, I decide to see what I can glean from her, but I don't know where to start. Is there a start?

I decide to start with the people. "So, there're not just people from Earth in this colony?"

"No." I wait for her to fill the silence. "There are four different races represented here."

"Four?"

"Ceres is in a useful position for exploring your solar system. Think of it as a service station, a drop off for refueling, rest or just plain meeting up with old friends. The universe is busier than you think," she explains, a little snottily I feel.

"Why have we never met any of these people?"

She stops and turns to me. "Why do you think? You Earth people can't get on with your own kind. Imagine what would happen if I turned up with a "Hi, you guys. I'm an Agamidonid, from Agamidonae. It's a planet in the constellation you call Cepheus." I'd be in a laboratory before my feet had touched the ground. I've seen the films."

She has a point. In fact the more I think about it the more I wonder if there are laboratories full of people from other planets, languishing as they await examination. The thought makes me shiver. I quickly move on.

"So, who else is here?" I ask. "You mentioned The Caputa is from somewhere that sounds spidery. Who is she?"

"The Caputa is an Arak from Arak-tan. Noah might not like me telling you this, but she is the President of the United Federation of Planets and very important."

"That sounds like something from a film," I chuckle.

"It's not funny," Nan snaps. "The Federation was formed to protect the friendly planets. They all work together for the good of their people. Sharing resources and scientific breakthroughs and the like. The Arak-tans were the first to conquer the problem of the enormous space distances. Those of us who would listen learnt from them. Those who wouldn't are jealous so despise them. She has her enemies and was hiding from one in particular when this catastrophe happened. Attercliffe is half Arak and half human."

"How come? I mean, nothing of this ever reaches the Earth colonies."

"How good's your memory?"

"Better but not brilliant," I tell her.

"Your parents' team was not the first to land here. Another team had been sent previously. Everything was going as planned until they had their own "Setback.""

I stare at her. "The *powers-that-be* knew nasty things could happen but still sent us?'

"You'd still be Earth-bound if you paid attention to every little blip. It was pirates, that time."

"Pirates?"

"There are pirates in all walks of life. They make life interesting."

"You have a very warped sense of semantics."

"To cut a long history short, the pirates attacked the colony and the Araks attacked the pirates. They sent them packing and all survivors settled down to live happily ever after. Then your colony came along and spoilt it."

"Phuddle," I cry. I don't want to believe that.

"It was fine at first, but people from Earth are so greedy. Anyway — it's all space dust now." She turns and waves to a small group of people heading our way.

"So you think the "Setback" was our own fault?" I am indignant but feel deep down that she might have a point.

"I'm afraid so."

"And we're all greedy?" I keep pushing it.

"No. I didn't say *all*. Well, I didn't *mean* all. We wouldn't be helping you if we ..."

"Oh? What happened here?" I gaze around me.

"Here?"

"There are no towers. Were they too badly damaged?" We had turned a corner and I indicate the wide-open space before us. The ground is tilled but nothing is growing in it. No grass or flowers.

"There never were towers here," Nan tells me. "This is an Agricultural Dome. There are a few towers to house the workers and the rest is farmland. Come, I have some people I want you to meet. They'll show you."

"THERE YOU ARE. We were worried about you." Braithe looks anxiously at us as we clatter into the Refectory.

"Sorry. We didn't realize the time," Nan tells her nonchalantly. We throw ourselves ungracefully into chairs. Nan shakes the teapot. "Janet?"

"Janet's finished for the day. She was worried because you didn't take anything for lunch."

"At least it gave her something useful to worry about." Nan heaves herself out of her seat and heads for the kitchen, teapot in hand.

Braithe shakes her head. "Noah was hoping to see you before he took his report to The Caputa."

"Nothing to report. Everything quiet." Nan throws the words over her shoulder before disappearing through the kitchen door.

"Nan shouldn't have kept you out so long after your ordeal yesterday," Braithe remarks.

"Oh, I'm fine," I tell her. "We had a lovely day. We just wandered through the fields and had a look at the intensive arable sheds. They are amazing!" I enthused. "Nan named the produce growing. We had lunch with a family who live over the other side of the dome. They have quite a sizeable farm. The ..." I pause to think.

"The Phillips?" she prompts. I nod. "Good. They're a good family."

"Are there many people living here?" I ask.

"Too few I'm afraid." She shrugs and then carries on. "This building is the Administrative and Social centre for the dome as well as being The Caputa's home. Janet and Attercliffe live in an apartment on the ground floor."

"Oh? Are they connubial?"

"Not officially but they do live together as such."

"Can Attercliffe speak? Only I've never heard him."

"If he has something to say. He understands well enough but doesn't speak much English. Janet translates for him. There are other buildings with people who are doing vital work enhancing our technology. You'll get to meet them over time — if you decide to stay. And the farm workers of course. We've had to go back to basics and it's hard work."

"Who else lives in this tower then, besides Nan and myself?"

"Well, on the same floor as you there's Noah and I, and Noah's younger brother ..."

Oh goody, goes through my mind.

"... Jared. You'll meet him eventually. The Caputa lives on the top floor with Cerberus and Gofor Nils as you know ..."

"Are they the two I met when I first arrived?"

"Indeed. Cerberus is a kind of guard. Noah called him that as a joke, but it stuck. His real name is quite unpronounceable. He's a Darnip from some distant planet you have yet to catalogue. Young Nils is a human and is a messenger cum dogsbody, hence the name — Gofor."

"So there's a spare room in this tower?"

"No." A long, slow intake of breath. "That room belongs to Libby."

"I've not seen her — have I?"

"No. Libby is on a mission." She pauses as if not sure what to say next. "You should know that Libby is — was — Sanderson's mother."

I am prevented from thinking of a suitable reply by the return of Nan with a fresh pot of tea and a plate of sandwiches. She puts them down in the middle of the table. "Janet left some stew. Come and help me carry stuff, Jax. Don't expect to be waited on here."

I cast a rueful look in Braithe's direction as I get up and follow Nan into the kitchen.

•   •   •

There's no sign of Noah's brother at breakfast in the morning. In fact, there's no sign of anyone. I'm still struggling with the time difference, but I like to be up early anyway. It's quiet in the dining area but I can hear Janet in the kitchen. I help myself to a plate of pastries and a pot of tea and sit down as Noah walks in and takes his customary place.

"What do you think of the setup?" Noah asks as he takes a pastry from my plate without so much as a bye-your-leave.

"How many domes are up and running?" I ask, glaring at him. He takes no notice at my attempt at making him uncomfortable.

"Just two farm domes are at their full potential. A third is getting there."

"I haven't seen food like this in the Admin Domes," I say, indicating the pastries.

"We grow everything ourselves and would willingly help the other domes, but they refuse us access. They think we're contaminated."

"So, what are they eating?"

"I have no idea. I believe there were supplies in the PolliPauz."

"Excuse me?"

"The PolliPauz is the name given to the Intergalactic Service Station on the other side of this rock. The English version anyway. You've not heard of it?"

I shake my head. I'm beginning to realize that I have a lot to learn about life on this small rock. "Surely that survived the "Setback" if it's on the other side of the planet."

"It was damaged. That's why we can't be sure about the cause of the blast. We used it for parts at the time."

I consider this as I drink my tea. "This tea has a nice taste. Different from the stuff we get in our domes." I don't want to hear about disasters.

"We grow the tea bushes. It's fresh."

"Have you anything for me to do today?" I ask, as I'm not used to doing nothing, of being so unregulated.

"That depends. Are you going to stay with us, or do you want to go back?"

"I'd like to stay." I want to speak to Libby Sanderson. I also want a look at Noah's brother, which is probably not the best of reasons for deciding to stay, but who cares.

"Good. We'll find you a role. But you had better stay close for the first few days. The Controllers will be looking for you."

That shakes me up a little. I know I should be expecting it. Every move you make is monitored within the domes. "The Caputa took my implant."

"That doesn't mean they don't know where you are. There's nowhere else to go when you think about it."

I try to find some information that will make me feel safer. "Will they venture this far? If they think we're contaminated?"

"We can't be sure, but they will send a party out in bio-suits. How long they look will depend on how important they think you are. Are you important?"

I shake my head, but I have another, deeper concern. "I don't think they'll forget."

"If they get too close, we'll release the Beasts."

I hardly dare ask but am too curious not to. "What Beasts are these?"

"Perhaps you'd like to visit the cages today?" Noah suggests. "I'm sure Nan will take you. She needs to stay close as well if you're right about the Controllers not forgetting."

Nan appears. "What's this? Who's taking my name in vain?"

"Good morning, Nan. I was just telling Jax that you might like to take her to meet the Beasts."

"Really?" she counters as she pours herself some tea from my pot. She doesn't sound very enthusiastic.

"You can't go back into the Admin Domes yet, and Jax would welcome the tour."

Nan looks at me and scowls. I smile back.

"Good, that's settled." He turns to his notes. There will obviously be no discussion.

I don't think Nan is too pleased about it, but after she has finished her breakfast, she rises to her feet and inclines her head, inviting me to follow.

•   •   •

"What Beasts are these?" I ask again as soon as we are clear of the tower.

"They came with the Darnips," Nan informs me. "They used them for fighting."

"What are they like?"

"Huge, scaled insects, I suppose is the nearest. They're difficult to describe to humans."

I shudder and ignore the quip. I look around me. "There's none loose in here. I hope."

Nan looks around too. "We catch them if we can and cage them for our own safety."

"Do they have claws?"

"Huge pincers and sharp teeth. Why do you ask?"

"Sanderson," I whisper. I can't get used to them being siblings.

"They have long canines. If Sanderson was torn to pieces, then you can bet your life it was a Beast. So, they got into your dome." She says it as a statement.

"Must have." Scary. "Do they have a name?"

Nan looks sideways at me as if I'm a pixel short of a picture. "Name? We don't name the Beasts."

"I don't mean like you would a pet. They must belong to some genus. Don't they have a name? Like cow or horse?" I name two animals I've heard of. "So you can identify them?"

"Oh. They're not that sort of creature. They were developed by the Darnips. The Darnips are an ancient race who like a bit of a ruckus but don't like getting hurt themselves. They developed the Beasts to take on the fight."

"Why are they here?"

"The Darnips?"

"No, the Beasts," I sigh.

"They are remarkably good at getting loose. Some got left behind when we dispelled their owners. I mean, Cerberus is okay, but some of them go over the top when spoiling for a fight. We couldn't have more than one or two Darnips together. They'd fight their own shadows if there was no one else about." I had to giggle at that, but Nan was serious. She carries on as if I hadn't interrupted. "Sometime in the past, the pirates harnessed any Beasts they came across and now use them to take on their own fights. Here we are."

We have arrived at a long low building built from reclaimed blocks. It's not far from the towers and I wonder if it's safe. The blocks the towers are built from are not that substantial. The dome is our protection. We have no need of heavy blocks and certainly no capacity on the SpaceBus for carrying the number we would need for a comfortable living. The outer door is unlocked, and we enter a dark corridor lit only by tiny windows. I follow Nan down the corridor until she reaches a junction. She indicates the left-hand turn and we continue until we come to another door. This one is locked at the top and the bottom.

Nan seems reluctant to open it. "They are caged?" I ask.

"Oh yes." She takes a deep breath and presses her thumb against the locking panels, one after the other. With a familiar beep, the door opens. She enters cautiously with me close behind.

I am expecting an animal smell, acrid and foul. There is almost no smell from the creatures. The Beasts themselves take my breath away. There are three and they are caged behind the same transparent substance used to make the domes. I lean back against the walkway wall, afraid that they will break through at any given moment. They are huge for insects, about the size of a large dog, and heavily built. They remind me of the creatures I see on my TP; the ones that survive anything from a nuclear war to a "Setback." Cockroaches, I think they're called. Their heads are heavy and scarily human, jutting from under a shield-like exoskeleton, with great hinged jaws from which sharp hooked canines hang. Pointed tusks protrude like javelins from either side of their snouts. The worst thing about them is that their carapace is mirrored, and I could imagine that once out on the surface of the planet they would reflect their surroundings and not be seen until it was too late.

"That's enough." I manage to step back outside where I turn on Nan. "How on Ceres could they have got inside our dome without being seen? Even with the mirrored carapace?"

"Come, I'll show you." Nan takes me along the corridor to another door. "They come in different sizes." She opens the door using her handprint and we enter a smaller compound. The Beasts here are nowhere near as large, and when they lie still in a corner of the stall, they are all but invisible. "These have a better cloaking device," she explains. "We presume the different sizes are for different tasks. I believe the pirates used to swagger about with the smaller ones. The others would be too much of a liability."

"Are these the young of the larger ones?" I ask. It seems obvious, but then again lots of things seemed obvious a few days ago.

"No. They don't breed. They are a manufactured creature, albeit partially organic."

"Can you be sure of that?" I am a tad apprehensive.

"I don't think anyone would stake their life on it but we're pretty sure. There has been no evidence so far. They sleep and feed and defecate. Just no urge to procreate as far as we can tell."

"Who looks after them?" I say as I press my nose up against the glass of their pen.

"My dad and Jared — with a bit of help. Dad is the scientist in charge. He does most of the experiments and research. Jared is his assistant. They have help, should they need backup."

I shudder. "What do you feed them on?" I'm not sure I want to know the answer but ask anyway.

Nan hesitates and then says quite simply, "Meat." She says it in a tone which does not inspire further questions.

"What shall we do now?" I ask in a voice too bright for the occasion.

I turn to leave as the door opens and a surly looking teenager slouches in. He barely gives eye contact as he nods in our direction. He presses his thumb on a keypad and unlocks the door of a cupboard set into the wall behind the door.

"Oh, good morning to you too, Jared. I'm very well, thank you for asking," flips Nan. Then, "Jared this is Jax. The Caputa approves. Jax, this rude bastard is Jared, Noah's brother."

I flinch at what she says.

"It's okay. Jared knows I'm only joking," Nan tells me.

I'm not used to this kind of repartee, and I'm not convinced she's joking. Things are very orderly in the Admin Domes. I would most likely be admonished for speaking to someone like that, even BJ.

The youth speaks. "Watch your mouth, Nan."

"Why? Will you tell your big brother? I'm so scared." Nan flings back.

Jared is not as tall or powerfully built as his brother, and he spoils what physique he has by hunching his shoulders. His colouring is nondescript, whereas Noah's is strong, and as he turns to look at Nan my eyes are immediately drawn to a cluster of teenage pimples around his nose and on his chin. His greasy hair is long and droops over his face, partially hiding his sour expression.

So much for Noah's brother.

"I have to get on," he mutters and pushes past Nan and begins to open the pen door.

"Come on, Jax. We'll leave the lad to his pets." She catches my arm and all but drags me out. "We'll go see if Dad's about."

•   •   •

Nan's dad is lovely. Facially he is serpentine in appearance and has a long slim body but basically he's humanoid, and I can see a resemblance in Nan. She is altogether more human-looking, and I wonder if Sanderson's mother is really her mother too, or whether her father has a partiality for human ladies.

"Call me Tadz," he invites as we are introduced. "Nanz does." He hisses slightly as he speaks which makes him quite endearing.

"Zo, you're going to join uz. Good, good. The Caputa approvez. We need new bloodz." He looks at me over his spectacles.

As I return the greeting, I notice a pen balancing precariously behind his very tiny ear and a test tube in his lab coat pocket. I can't take my eyes from the test tube as it's steaming, and he doesn't appear to notice. He sees me looking though.

"Take no notizz of that," he tells me patting his pocket gently. "I'm conducting an experiment and it needz to be kept warm."

"Haven't you a lab?" I ask.

"Oh yesss but that Jared'z a bit of a liability. It zeems safer to keep it here. Now, what about a cup of tea?" We follow him into his laboratory which appears rather basic after the labs in the first domes, but Tadz seems happy with it.

Over the tea and some of Janet's homemade biscuits, which I expect to be sweet but actually taste a tad herby although not unpleasant, Tadz explains his work. It appears his job is not to shut down the creatures, but to find a way of adapting them for use.

"You zee, they're very ztrong. Ztronger than the horsez and can do more work in lezz time."

"You have horses for work?"

I know some people in my dome like to ride horses for pleasure, but I'd never heard of using them for work. The first horses were brought as embryos, stored cryogenically along with those of cows, sheep and some petting animals. Some of the scientists research how they cope with life under the domes on this planet. If their introduction is successful, it's another step nearer to colonizing Ceres in a sustainable way.

"Much of the machinery waz destroyed, but even if we had mechanical means, fuel is nearly impossible to get. We began using the horses from the riding zchool to help with the heavy work and found it zuited our temperamentz. It zavez on our limited ztock of fuel, and they provide manure for the fieldz. We have found a uze for everything. We had to." He takes a long swallow of his tea, eyeing me from behind the rim of the cup. "What do you know, Jax?"

He seems very perceptive, or is it just part of his make-up? I know nothing about the Agamidonid.

"One of those creatures got into my dome and killed my friend ..." I am about to add Sanderson's name, but suddenly remember that he is his father and stop. I don't know what he knows but I don't want to be the one to tell him if he is unaware.

"Zo I've been told," Tadz says quietly. "He waz my zon."

I nod. "Nan told me. I'm sorry for your loss." I add lamely. I remain quiet, not sure how to carry on.

Tadz leans forward and pats my knee as if I am the one needing comfort. "Libby Zanderson began working here before the "Zetback." That'z when we met. The Agamidonid are not a monogamouz raze. and Nanz's mother, Marzie and I were going through a rough patch because of thiz. To cut a long ztory short, Libby fell pregnant with Jaimz and she, Marzie, myzelf, and the children all lived together in some sort of harmony for a while. I encouraged the women to look to other malez, but they were not uzed to that lifestyle. Although Marzie iz now living with a farmer on the other zide of the dome."

"How come Sanderson was living in my dome?" I ask.

"Both Jaimz and Nanz are — were — very human to look at. Jaimz in particular, zo we zlipped him into the dome az a zpy."

"Aren't they sussed? The spies? I mean, we're monitored all the time." I have been scared of not watching the television feed as it has been commented on in my reviews. How on Ceres did they manage to infiltrate the Admin domes without it being picked up?

"People are moved about all the time. Surely you've notized?" He eyes me quizzically. "Then you're not very old. Libby was reazzigned to the Admin Dome just before the "Zetback" and was working on the PDB. Once she realized that thingz weren't what they should be, she ensured she ztayed on the databaze. She's a brilliant hacker. She managez her own electronic information in order to be where she needz to be at any given time. She alzo calibratez the chipz we inject into our zpiez in order that they are not identified by the Controllerz." He muses a little before continuing. "She haz proved invaluable in inputting any data we need. She input a detailed persona for Jaimz." He saw me staring at him. "What?"

"Wasn't Jaimz with Libby in the Admin Dome?" I asked.

"No, he stayed with me and Marzie. He waz zettled, you zee. Anyway, Libby provided him with a file on the PDB, he zlipped in through the tunnels, kept a low profile for three dayz and, Bob'z your uncle: Fanny'z your aunt. He waz in." He sees me staring at him. "What?"

"Bob's your uncle; Fanny's your aunt?" I ask.

"An Earth zaying?" He queries. "You muzt know it. It's one of my favoritez."

I shake my head. I don't know it.

"It'z a hobby of mine. Collecting old zayingz from Earth. The older the better."

We are moving away from the subject so instead of answering I tell him, "The Controllers don't forget in the same way as most people." A thought has just occurred to me. "What if they had sussed Sanderson and let the Beast in on purpose to get rid of him?"

"Do you think it possible?" Nan looks worried. "We have other people there."

"It could well be pozzible," Tadz considers. "I would go and tell Noah immediately. Libby'z in DN1 now." He sounds concerned.

Nan throws the rest of her tea down her throat and pulls me from my seat. "Come on. This is important. See you, Dad."

WHEN WE ARRIVE, Noah is talking to two people I have not seen before, but that doesn't stop Nan, who bursts into the Refectory and the conversation. Noah looks up crossly and a wave of irritation crosses his face.

"This is important, Noah." Nan tells him sharply. "A matter of life and death." There is no "sorry". "Is Libby back yet? Jax is concerned that we may have been rumbled."

A look of fear crosses Noah's face but he controls it. "No, she's not. How come?" He waves away the people he had been talking to and turns to me.

"I am sure that Sanderson was killed by one of the Beasts," I tell him. "I'm wondering whether, as the Controllers don't forget, they had him killed to prevent him passing on information." I will seriously have to reconsider my notion of Sanderson. I always thought of him as a little wimp. Perhaps that was the persona he adopted in order to be overlooked by the SET.

"She has a point," Nan urges.

"Are any of our Beasts missing?" Noah asks as he checks details on his technopad.

"No. Dad would have reported it if there was. In case they were loose in the dome."

Noah agrees. "We need more information. Especially about the forgetfulness."

"We need to get Libby out," snaps Nan.

"No. First, I need to go back." I say the words bravely but am secretly hoping they will say 'no'. They don't.

"Would you do that?" Noah asks gently.

I nod because I don't trust myself to speak. I clear my throat, "It was something Nan said earlier. I think it might be the food."

"The food?" Noah asks.

"The Refectory food. It seems the most logical. The food in the Refectories is eaten by everyone except the Controllers. It's free at source so most people just fill up with it. The Controllers have their own eating establishments. Plus — I ate very little. I stocked up on snacks, which anyone can buy, Controllers included. My friend BJ eats loads of Refectory food and he seems to forget very quickly." My throat feels tight as I thought of him wolfing down the supposingly nutritious stuff they served us.

"You certainly make a good case. Could you formulate a plan using the information you have about the dome?" Noah is all attention.

"There's no need for a plan. I'll sneak in and steal some food. Your dad can test it, can't he?" I ask of Nan.

"Sounds like a plan to me," she says, "but it's not been long since you left. The Controllers will still be on guard."

"I could wait," I say expectantly.

"We don't have that luxury," decides Noah. "You must leave as soon as you can."

"There is the time difference," I say hopefully.

"They are roughly five Earth hours in front of us. If you set off first thing on our tomorrow you'll have all day to get there. You may have to wait in the tunnel until it's a good time …"

"Or she may be lucky and get in when it's quiet," chips in Nan.

"Will you come with me?" I ask Nan. "We can look for Libby while we're there."

"You're better going alone," Noah warns me as Nan nods in agreement. "Plus I want you in and out as quickly as possible. There's going to be no more going to the Admin Domes until we know about the food."

"You'll be less conspicuous without me," Nan tells me.

"Having that information will inform any further plans we will make," Noah continues as if uninterrupted.

I have a big mouth but for some strange reason I feel responsible for Sanderson's mother even though I've never met her. Her son was my friend. I need to do this for her.

"What about Libby?" I ask.

"Libby's a big girl," Noah tells me. "She can look after herself."

•　　　•　　　•

Only Noah, Nan and Janet are up to see me off. Janet has packed me enough food for a week. She doesn't want me to have to eat or drink anything provided in the Admin Dome in case my theory is true. I am hopefully not going to be that long. It is my intention to be in and out before anyone registers that I am there at all. I shall take a small amount of food from the nearest Refectory and hurry back as if one of the Beasts is on my tail.

I have one of the uniforms of the Admin Domes in my rucksack. It appears these people have a selection ready for their spies. Braithe brought it to my room the night before and I shall change in the tunnel before I enter DN 2. It's a little on the loose side but fits me well enough. The dust in the damaged domes is black and sticky, as well as having the possibility of it being contaminated. It would not do to enter the dome dirty.

That will be noticed as everything is so sanitised there. She also lightened my hair a little, and painted my face so it looks like I have a small scar on my cheek. I am surprised at the difference. I shall not be immediately recognised, and without my old chip it will take time for the computer system to identify my DNA. I have not been fitted with a false chip, as I am told it takes a while for the computers to register differences and I do not intend being there long enough for that. Components are in short supply and only used where absolutely necessary.

In, grab some food, and out; that's the plan.

I am worried about losing my way in the damaged domes, as there are no landmarks to guide me, but Noah hands me a technopad. "It has been wiped and re-calibrated," he tells me. "You are quite safe carrying it. It will show you the way across the domes and you will be able to keep in touch with us."

He leans over and switches on the TP. I smell apple soap and a slight muskiness. I see a little green dot sitting on an illuminated line.

"That's you. I have the same on mine. We will know where you are at all times. The TP contains a tracker. Follow the illuminated line and you will be fine. If you are in trouble press this button," he indicates the one. "The dot will turn red and we will be alerted. Find a safe place and stay put. One of us will come for you. Providing it is safe to do so."

I am disturbed by the last remark, but I am dismissed, so with no more excuses, Nan and I head for the exit.

My friend escorts me to the door from this dome into the inspection corridor. I was rather hoping she would surprise me by telling me she will come most of the way with me, but she doesn't. At the exit Nan takes my pad and looks closely at it. I see a route marked out on the screen as she hands it back. "Just make sure you keep to the route," she reminds me. She pauses and then, "Hurry back," before turning away in embarrassment.

I start off confidently enough, as my way is determined by the tunnel. It is lit now. Although not very bright, it is better than nothing. A soft shuffle stops me in my tracks. I flatten myself against the wall, although how I think that will hide me, I don't know. A shadow falls across the tunnel and I hold my breath in the hope that I will not be detected.

"It's alright," says a soft voice. "It's only me."

I let out my breath and almost snap at the figure that stands in my way.

"What are you doing? You scared me to death."

"Hardly," comments Braithe dryly.

"You know what I mean. Are you coming with me?" I ask hopefully.

"No. Well, not all the way. My journey takes me along the same route for most of it."

"Where are you going?" I ask.

"You must have a lot of questions." Braithe changes the subject; obviously not a "need to know".

I do have many questions but don't know where to start. "I have more about the set-up in Domes 1 and 2, really," I tell her. "I think that, in the long run, it will affect us all."

"You're probably right," she agrees. "Testing the food will answer some of our questions for a start, though."

"I don't like the food," I tell her. "I think it has a funny after-taste. I eat a lot of snacks. The snacks are different. Sanderson ate a lot of snacks."

"Perhaps he had the same thought as you," she says.

Braithe sets a grueling pace, and we jog on in silence for a while and soon reach the end of the dome. I am beginning to struggle, and she must see that, as we take the tunnel at a much more relaxed pace. We chat about this and that and I tell her about the small likenesses I keep to remind me of my family. She seems impressed. She tells me that she was employed as an agricultural scientist and her specialism was making the grain crop more productive, but what she's really interested in is seeing if it is possible to plant enough trees to alter the atmosphere on Ceres.

At the entrance to the final dome, I will have to cross, Braithe stops. "I shall have to leave you now. My way is not your way. Before I go can I ask a favour? You may say no. It will not be held against you."

I wonder where she can be going from that point but instead of asking I quip with a frivolity I don't feel, "That sounds ominous."

In answer she takes a small piece of paper from a hidden pocket and passes it to me. I turn it around and around in my hand. "How was this made?"

"It's called a photograph. You need a specially adapted TP to take it. You don't have photography in your domes?"

"No. There are no likenesses allowed. If it was known I had any, I would be in serious trouble."

She points towards the paper. "That is Libby Sanderson."

"She looks a lot like you," I stare at Braithe.

"She's my sister." She pauses for a moment and I see her face working as she struggles to control her emotions. "If you see her, could you bring her back?"

I nod. I take another look at the photograph, but I don't really need it. I just need to look for someone who looks like Braithe. "Of course." I pass it back to her and she takes it too quickly to be polite. It obviously means a lot to her.

"Don't put yourself in danger," she warns. "Take care and good luck." She tucks the photograph back in her pocket and disappears into the gloom.

Now I am truly alone and very, very scared.

I cross the dome slowly and then trudge through the final long tunnel. I have no wish to reach my destination, but for some reason the doorway appears much too quickly for my liking. I peer through. The way is lit and there are a huge number of people about. I try to work out the time using the information I have picked up on my travels. I imagine it is teatime, about four o'clock, in this dome, and some people are going back to their towers after their shift. Others will be on their way to work the evening shift, and yet others will be looking for some sort of recreation. It's very busy.

I change quickly and stow my rucksack. I'm ready for my task, I think.

ALL THE WAY THROUGH the final tunnel, I have been hemming and hawing as to the best way to deal with my task. My mind is made up for me when I spot BJ in the crowd that has just left the mono-pod. He must have just finished his shift. My heart thuds at the sight of him. He might be a big daft lummox, but he personifies safety and normality. I want to rush up and hug him but instinctively know that it would cause a ruckus and I would not be able to complete my task. I decide that meeting with BJ is a good omen. He lives quite close to the mono-port for a start, and he lacks any sense of curiosity. He is chatting to someone on the platform. I sidle out of the tunnel and step into the crowd.

"BJ?'

He swings round. "Who are you?" There is no recognition in his eyes. He just looks puzzled. He nods to his friend, who disappears into the crowd of people leaving the mono-port.

Alone with BJ, I nearly lose it and cry out my name, but swallow it back. "I used to work with you, back in the day," I lie. When he doesn't answer I add, "Have you forgotten me already?" He stands with his mouth open.

BJ thinks with his belly. "I'm on my way to tea."

I smile as benignly as I can. "Can I come with you? I haven't had my tea yet."

He hesitates. I swallow and stare at him willing him to say something.

"I don't know you. What do you want?"

People are starting to notice us and look in our direction.

I panic and start to stammer. "Sorry. Sorry. I thought you were someone else." I turn and hurry away from him. The crowd resumes its pattern behind me like water swirling behind the boats on the park lake. I lose myself in the crowd and exit the mono-port without thought of where I am going.

People in the Admin Domes walk with purpose but without rushing, so hurrying at this pace begins to attract attention. I will myself to slow down and act as normally as I can. Looking about me, I find myself standing outside my old tower, the last place I feel I need to be. BJ didn't recognize me, but someone might. I feel my heart beating painfully in my chest, my breathing labored, and any sense of direction has deserted me, along with any problem-solving skills I may once have had.

I should have kept my head and gone inside to the Refectory, taken some food and then left. I wouldn't have stood out, as people don't stick to their own towers in order to eat. I could have completed my task and been on my way if I hadn't panicked. Instead, I keep moving along the street, as I am well aware that standing still will cause me to be noticed. Aimless wandering will also look suspect. Squaring my shoulders, I make an effort to look purposeful and head towards the nearest mono-port. It is not the one Nan and I used, but at the other end of DN 2. I hope to get into the tunnel there and hide while I reconsider my options. I am not a spy. I'm no good at this spying game. I don't know why I even suggested going myself. Surely they have someone else who could have done it.

The mono-port is quiet. People are now in their designated places for the evening making me very conspicuous, something I had not thought about. With my head down I make for the tunnel door, only to find it locked. I feel the panic rising again. I have to get out of the dome as soon as possible before my presence is picked up. I have no thought now of finding any food samples. I just need to get out and find safety.

"Well I never. Fancy seeing you here." The unfamiliar voice breaks into my consciousness. I swing round and stare at the woman who has spoken to me.

"Do I know you?" I query. As far as I know, I have never seen her before in my life but I suppose I could have. I am reminded of one of the small animals in the pictures they show us in the Education films. Rodents I think they're called; all pointy and crafty looking.

"Of course. Come with me." I hang back. "Do you want to be caught?" A snarled whisper. "You're putting us both in jeopardy.

"You're not Libby."

"Why? Would you go with her?"

I start to nod but the stranger continues, "You are putting us all in danger. Come with me."

She grabs my wrist and pulls me behind her, and I have no choice but to follow the stranger out of the mono-port and into the nearest tower. She drags me into the gym, which is deserted at this time.

"Don't get too comfortable. You're no safer here than out there," she snaps.

I croak, "Who are you?" I am just out of my depth and plain scared.

"A friend from another dome. Noah is concerned."

I relax a little; didn't Noah say he would know if I was in trouble? Her gaze bores into me as if she could read my mind. I don't even think about using the technopad to see what color the dot is. But if she is from Noah ...

"It's all gone wrong," I tell her. "I was supposed to sneak in, grab some of the Refectory food and sneak out again before being noticed."

"Is that all?"

"Is that all?"

I am aghast. "Is that *all*?"

"Okay, okay. Don't get your knickers in a twist. It doesn't sound like much to me."

"Well, it is to me," I snap. "The computers will have picked up my presence by now and Enforcement will be looking for me."

"Fortunately for you, the computers are not as quick as you think. Come with me. I'll pick up some supper and you can take it back with you." I stare at her. "Don't you trust me?"

"No," I snap. I am beginning to recover my equilibrium or at least making the effort.

"If I was going to turn you in, I would have done so already."

"What if you wanted me followed in order to catch the rest of the people in the damaged domes?" I throw back at her.

"If I was a grass for Security Enforcement, I wouldn't know about the other domes. It is put about that everyone perished. It's need-to-know."

She has the words, but somehow, I'm not convinced. It may be put about for the workers, but the Controllers are a different matter.

"You could be a spy," I counter.

"Look this is getting us nowhere. Every minute you are here is increasing the danger of you getting caught and me with you."

"In that case I'll go." Her attitude is putting my back up and helps me to get on top of my panic and put on a brave face.

"Alone?"

"Alone. I'll get the food and go back without your help, thank you." I don't want to let Noah and the others down.

"Let me check that there is no one about before you go." She goes to the door.

Am I a fool for trusting her? I feel my heart lift into my throat as she does so. I am trapped here. There is no other way out, and if she is opening the door to Enforcement, I am done for. My vision tunnels as she peers out and my stomach cramps in fear. So much for conquering the panic.

"Okay, let's go."

There is no one there. I realize that not only am I shaking, but I haven't drawn a breath until that moment. I gulp in air before I follow her out.

"Aren't you going for food?" She looks towards the Refectory.

"No. I'll go elsewhere," I snap contrarily and turn towards the exit.

The tower seems deserted, and as we step outside, I see the street is quiet.

At the bottom of the steps, she stops and points to her left. "Follow this street until you come to T 10, take a left and you'll find the mono-port in front of you. If you're hungry you could get some supper in the tower before you go." Her tone is conversational, and she takes my hand and shakes it as if I have been a visitor and she is seeing me off.

"Thank you …" I hesitate. I don't know her name. She smiles and turns away before melting among the buildings. I don't think she goes back inside the building we have just left.

What if she is a spy and is waiting for me to lead the Security Team back through the tunnels? I hesitate for too long. My reverie is shattered by a friendly voice calling my name.

"Hey, Jax?"

Involuntarily I turn. Another mistake. Two Enforcement officers emerge from the nearest towers. I put down my head and run.

I have no plan, just instinct. I run into the nearest Tower and through the dining area. It is full of people getting their evening meal and I hope to lose myself in the crush. I crash into someone and warm soup splashes across my chest and soaks through my tunic, making me gasp. I race on, dodging and swerving. My ploy seems to be working as people stand, trays in hands, and stare, blocking the way for my pursuers. All the time, I am swearing at myself for trusting a total stranger.

I bolt into the kitchens and down the back stairs and out through the service doors. I find myself in an enclosed yard, which contains the food bins at the end of the waste chute. I open the gate leading into the back street, but there is no way I can outrun the Team for long. I double back and climb onto one of the bins, and slip inside the one next to it and squelch down among the waste food. I have barely pulled the lid shut after me when I hear the Enforcement Team crashing through the doors after me. Someone shouts about the gate and they all rush through.

I stay among the oozing waste for a long, long time; too scared to get out. I hope against hope that the bin won't be sucked empty while I'm still inside. I have forgotten about the tracker still in my pocket and feel my heart squeeze in my chest when I hear someone close by whisper my name.

"Jax? It's me, Braithe."

I cautiously lift the lid even though I recognise the voice. She asks no questions, just stands by as I clamber out. She leads me through the shadows towards the mono-port, which is now deserted as it is getting quite late. We slide through the maintenance doors and set off at a cracking pace.

"What happened?" Braithe slows when we reach the first of the Industrial Domes and we walk through at an easy pace.

"Someone claimed to know me. I thought it might be Libby at first, but she looked nothing like."

"Thin, dark, this tall?" Braithe lifts her hand to just above her shoulder.

"Yes. She had cruel eyes."

"Romney."

"Pardon?"

"Romney. Her name's Romney. She has been compromised. I don't think she knows which side she's on anymore."

"How do you mean compromised?"

"She was caught some time ago and brainwashed by Enforcement. It doesn't seem entirely successful, but they are obviously using her."

"I didn't get any food."

Braithe laughs. "Have you seen yourself? You're covered in food. There's more than enough sticking to you for Tadz to test."

I am exhausted by the time we get back and all I want to do is go straight to my room but first they insist I shower and change in the gym. Braithe follows me and takes the food-stained clothes as soon as I shed them.

I take a long hot shower, washing away the disappointment of my behavior while on this mission before heading to my room and falling into bed. I don't even manage the plate of sandwiches Nan has brought me from the kitchen.

THE MOOD AROUND the breakfast table the next morning is subdued. Libby is still missing, and we are in limbo waiting for the test results on the food. I feel a failure even though I completed my mission, as it was more through luck than any derring-do on my part.

Nan keeps asking me what happened, how did I come to be in the bin, was it exciting? I get snappy with her because I don't want her to know how scared I was and that I got the food by accident. In the end, she leaves me alone and goes to see how her father is getting on with the tests.

I want to know what is going on; why there is so much animosity between the two groups. It can't just be the fact that there might be contamination by now, but no one is saying anything, and I don't feel up to asking. I'm scared they'll tell me. I'm scared I'm a failure and Noah will send me back.

The tests seem to take forever, but in fact it's only a little over 24 hours. Noah stops me from leaving the supper table with the others. Braithe slides round and sits beside me.

"Tadz has the test results," Noah informs me. "You were right. There is a chemical in the food. It's a form of Midazolam, but it's been extensively modified, otherwise you'd all be asleep."

"Everyone seems quite slow in their reactions," I admit. I hadn't thought about it before, but then I'd had nothing to compare it to. I wonder why they have waited for everyone else to go before telling me that. The idea was for that information to help us decide what to do next. Braithe takes my hand.

"There's more," Noah continues. I look from one to the other. What on Ceres could they have discovered? "The food contains the DNA of sapient beings …" He pauses and takes a deep breath. "Human beings — in the main. Well — human DNA actually." He doesn't give me eye contact, his mouth tight with emotion.

Everything seems to recede.

"Are you alright?" Braithe pats my hand. "You've gone very pale."

My vision swims and she pushes my head between my knees, where I throw up everything I've just eaten.

"Sorry," I croak, wiping my mouth on the back of my hand.

"Don't worry. It has been a shock to us all. Come on, I'll help you get cleaned up. We can talk when you are feeling better."

I stand shakily. My boots and trouser legs are splashed with vomit and I am reluctant to spread it further.

Janet appears; she must have been waiting. "Get along, Noah. Leave us to the lass." Her tone does not invite argument, and Noah reluctantly disappears. She helps me out of my top clothes and wraps a blanket around me. Braithe takes my arm, and we head towards my room, leaving Janet to clean up.

I don't leave my room for two days after the news. Nan and Janet leave tempting things outside my bedroom door, but other than grudgingly answering their pleas as to whether I'm okay, I have nothing to do with anyone. I'm afraid to eat, even though I know the food is organically grown. Thoughts swim around and around in my head until it aches. I am restless and exhausted at the same time. What if I ate Sanderson? Someone will have eaten Sanderson. I know I have to deal with this, but I haven't the energy.

Eventually, Braithe insists I get up. She stands by while I shower and dress before revealing chocolate.

"It's real," she says as she places it on the table.

"I thought you didn't have chocolate?" I mumble.

"Emergencies only. I lifted it when I went in to fetch you out," Braithe replies. "It's okay. It's Controller's chocolate. Noah's waiting for a word."

There is no "if you're up for it." I nod and follow her to a room in the basement.

The basement has been re-modelled. The laundry and storage lockers are still there, but I am right about the gym being smaller than the ones in Domes 1 and 2. In the space created, there is what appears to be an office, the walls lined with screens. Noah is sprawled in a chair staring at the screens.

"Hey," quips Braithe as we enter. She drops into a chair by a table covered with papers and a tray of tea and pastries. She indicates that I do the same.

Noah swings round and stares at me. "I'm sorry about springing that info on you," he says. "It's obvious you had no idea."

I shake my head. I don't trust myself to speak.

"Now we know where the food comes from."

"Do we?" I ask. "Who exactly are they using and why haven't we sussed it?"

"Well, obviously, you all forget things. You won't remember someone you worked with a few days after they've gone — even you." Noah reminds me. "Plus, some of you are moved around a lot, from what Libby tells me. Probably those who are less productive in some way. It will be a ploy, so you don't query why people go missing."

"Everyone I encounter when I'm in the Admin Domes is young. Roughly your age and certainly not much older than Noah and I." Braithe informs me.

I don't answer immediately. Although I have just had a thought about that, and it has shaken me more than anything else I've experienced over the past few days. I look from Noah to Braithe and clear my throat. I'm not sure where to start.

"You don't seem altogether surprised," Braithe says quietly.

"No. You see. You're right. There's no …" I think for a moment. "There's not much difference in ages. There're no old people like Tadz."

"You think Tadz is old?" Noah asks.

"Well, yes. He's older than anyone I've ever seen. Even the Controllers." They look at each other over my head. "Do you think we are dis-disposed of when we reach a certain age?" I whisper.

"Do you think it's possible?" Noah doesn't reassure me.

"What are we going to do?" I ask.

"We need more information, but the main outline is …"

"What information? Don't you have enough?" I almost scream at him.

"We have more than enough about what they are doing, but we have to know why. It can't go on and we need to know what we are up against. We can't just go barging in and tell them to stop it."

"We need to know who is behind it all, how many people are involved in the cover-up, how it all operates …" Braithe trails off. "Lots of things," she finishes lamely.

"Go and get something to eat," Noah says to me, regardless of the fact that there is both food and drink on the table.

I am obviously dismissed. I have so many questions. The more I find out, the less I seem to know.

I find Nan in the dining area. She is waiting for me and we wander outside and away from the buildings, to the orchard where the blossom is in bud. It is beautiful in the scented air and I find it difficult to believe Tadz's findings. I try to find the answer to some of my questions.

"How come there are different races, here, in this dome?"

"They were in the PolliPauz when you humans got here. Taking a break from inter-galactic dashing about. They helped, you know, with getting set up. Unfortunately, it wasn't appreciated," she said coldly.

"What do you mean?"

"Humans can't share. It's all mine, mine, mine, with you lot."

"Come on, Nan. We're not all like that."

"No. Sorry, you're not. Unfortunately, the *powers-that-be* are like that. That's how they get to be *powers-that-be*. There was some trouble among the different races, and The Caputa turned up at the same time looking for support. It was all a mess, and because of that no one can be sure what caused the 'Setback'."

Nan is right, and I am ashamed of my people a lot of the time. The grass beneath the fruit trees is sprinkled with small white flowers. I turn onto my stomach and take great interest in pulling a daisy apart rather than look at her.

"We all pulled together after the "Setback", and you can see the result. Everything's working and no one is eating anyone else."

That hurt, but she's right and I have no answer. Instead, I get to my feet.

"Where are you going?'

"Just a walk. By myself." I march off. I need to think.

THE LITTLE GOFOR BOY finds me as the sun is dimming. "Please, Jax, Noah has asked for you." His words are clipped and precise. As we wander back, the gofor boy tells me his name is Nils Vinke and his parents work the farmland in this dome. He has older brothers who help on the farm, and he finds the work for The Caputa easier for him and much more fun. He's quite a chatterer and gives me no opportunity for questions.

We walk into the tower to find there are a lot of people I have not met in the dining area. In fact, it is quite full, with all chairs taken and some folk standing. Nan indicates a seat she has saved beside her, and I slide in. Janet is also sitting instead of bustling about. I don't think I've ever seen her still for more than a few minutes.

I'm not the last; two more stretched men arrive dressed for the farm. Noah stands and surveys the room before laying out the ground rules.

"I think we're all here. I'll begin by explaining the situation as we know it and what we still need to know. I'll then invite ideas as to how we move forward. You are sitting at tables of six. Those standing form groups of six or thereabouts. Each group will be given time to discuss and consider. Elect a spokesperson to put your ideas forward. I want no shouting out." A few hands go up. "Questions afterwards, if I haven't already answered them by then."

•　　　•　　　•

I learn a few things from Noah's speech.

For example, contamination was a very real threat and a large number of people had died from exposure to chemicals and radiation in the early days, including Noah and Jared's mother. I do feel some sympathy with the other domes. Noah's father led the movement to reintegrate with the non-contaminated domes but ended up exhausted and disillusioned. He was eventually taken prisoner by the Controllers, and Noah hasn't heard any more of him. He presumes he is dead and took up the struggle, but the fight is very different today.

For a start, it is a fight that whoever is in overall charge of the Controllers does not want to acknowledge. They don't want to know us or care what happens to us. The aims of the Agricultural Domes are different too. The end result is expected to be the same — everyone reunited, working together, and eating food from the farms and not each other.

But, initially we have to bring down the establishment in Domes 1 and 2, and free the people from the police state. Noah's words — not mine.

The police state is safe and secure, and peaceful. It is safe and secure and controlling. We are controlled by some nameless, faceless entity until we are fat and tender. Then it is no longer safe and secure. It is deadly.

The meeting goes on into the night, until it is obvious that people are tiring, and ideas are going around in circles. Eventually, Noah brings proceedings to a halt, but we are expected to continue with our thoughts and reconvene the following evening.

However, we have achieved a list of aims agreed by all. We just need people to come up with a plan as to how to implement them.

•   •   •

When Noah surveys the room at the start of the next meeting, he sees a much more subdued group. Many are finding their TP's very interesting and some even have scraps of paper and are doodling. No one wants to give eye contact.

"Okay, everyone," Noah begins but he is interrupted immediately.

"Is this really necessary?" One of the stretched men lumbers to his feet. "Only how I see it is this. We are safe here. We're up and running and have food and systems for purifying water and replenishing the oxygen. Do we need the other domes?" There are a few nods and murmurs of agreement that rumble around the room.

Noah looks around as if finding the people wanting. Those who chose to give stares of defiance soon turn away. "You are right, Lenz. We could abandon our fight and put all our energy into completing the domes and farms. We could consider a manufacturing dome in the future. But do you really think that the Controllers would leave us alone? Especially when they see what we have achieved."

"They don't want to know us." Lenz continues. "They blocked our way. They think we're contaminated. They won't come here."

"They're already here," says Noah quietly.

The rumble becomes a roar. I flush with guilt even though I have nothing to be guilty of. I then realise that I have not seen Janet today, and Nan only fleetingly.

Everyone is clamouring for names or evidence, but Noah just raises his hand for silence. "It has been dealt with," he tells them. They'll soon find out. If it's not Janet, and I can't for one-minute think it is, it will be someone somebody knows, and the word will spread "They are monitoring our every move," he continues. "I've yet to find out why, but I will. In the meantime, we must continue the fight. I need volunteers."

The meeting breaks up, some people go back to their homes but quite a number approach Noah to enlist. I look for Nan and Janet.

Nan is sitting on the steps outside of the building. She looks upset. "Where's Janet?" I ask.

"Isn't she here?" Nan looks around but her cheeks are flushed, and she doesn't give me eye contact.

"No. It can't be Janet." I refuse to believe it.

"Shh. Come with me." Nan grabs my hand, and we hurry inside and back to her room.

As soon as the door shuts behind us, she swings around, her cheeks are flushed and there are tears in her eyes. "Braithe caught her this morning. She said she was cleaning in Noah's office, but the file she had been accessing would be very dangerous in the wrong hands. It hadn't finished shutting down. When Braithe asked her why that file was open, she couldn't answer. She's under guard now, Noah's tried questioning her, but apparently, she hasn't spoken since. Not even to Attercliffe.'

"Is he involved?"

"It doesn't appear so, but time will tell."

"But Janet ..." I don't know what else to say.

"Janet blames The Caputa for the "Setback." She's never denied that, but we thought she'd see sense over time. Get over it."

"Is The Caputa to blame?" I ask.

"I don't know. I was only a child. There was an argument involving her and the Principal Control over ownership."

"Ownership of what?"

"There you go. You don't question the idea of ownership. You expect it."

"What are you talking about, Nan? You said there was an argument over ownership, and I just wanted to know who owned, or thought they owned, what.

"No one owns anything. That was what the quarrel was about. You humans thought you could claim ownership of the planet, but The Caputa does not believe in one set of individuals owning land or any natural resource come to that. The planet and its resources are for use by all. No ownership. No arguments. End of."

"But — but how does that work?"

"I just give up. We share. Try it. It works."

"I'm sorry, but it's how we do it," I mutter in a subdued tone.

"It doesn't make it right," Nan snaps at me.

"I'll learn. I don't want us to fall out. I'm sorry."

"So am I." Nan sighs. "I liked Janet. It's floored Noah. I think Braithe had her suspicions for a while but she's still in shock."

"Do we know the damage she's caused?"

"That's not in our need-to-know."

"Are you sure? Don't we need to be on the lookout for anything amiss?"

"Probably but that's how it is at this moment."

"What's happened to her?"

"That's not in our need-to-know as well, so don't push it."

I shrug. I'll find out eventually I decide. "Can we do anything?"

"Well. We might. We need information like how many Controllers there are. Who's in charge now. How many Enforcement officers. Fancy a trip to Domes 1 and 2?"

I try to think of an argument, but Nan has all the answers.

"It's late. Too late to go tonight," I try.

"All the better. Noah would stop us if he knew. We need to go when no one would expect."

"But what about the time at the other end?"

"There's roughly five hours difference. It's half nine here now so it'll be around half two in the morning there. If we get a move on, we'll arrive just before the morning shift starts. We'll mix with the crowd — hidden in plain sight. We can be in and out."

"Uniforms. What about ..."

"There's some in the cupboard next to Noah's office. No probs."

"Aren't they locked?"

"No."

"What about the other end? We have no chips."

"I have," Nan retorts.

"Well, I haven't, and as soon as we try to hack the PDB the alarms will sound, and the doors will automatically lock, and we'll be — be turned into somebody's dinner — probably."

"*I* have the key."

"What key?"

"Libby's key." I was about to speak but Nan put her finger to her lips and shushed me. "I was with Braithe when she discovered Janet. She wasn't watching me, and I memorized the key code. It was just sitting there. Janet, silly mare, had written the codes down as she was downloading the files. She was so flustered at seeing Braithe that she left the paper on the desk. There was one for Noah's database and one for the PDB in DN 1. It's all here." She taps her head and grins. "Are you ready?"

"What if you've remembered it wrongly?"

"I haven't. You have to have nerves of steel and a brilliant memory if you're going to be a spy."

I shuddered as I remembered my ridiculous attempt at getting hold of some food the other day. She skips out of her room and towards the basement. I follow for two reasons. One, I want to prove I am an asset to this group, and two, I'm curious. Bloody nosy, you might say. Curiosity and cats spring to mind.

We escape without detection with nothing but the adapted TPs, a bottle of water, some of Janet's biscuits and two clean uniforms. Nan sets up a cracking pace. She would rather be there early and wait a short time than late and have to wait all day. So would I. I am worried that the computers will pick us up quickly enough whatever everybody else thinks.

It is a little over eighteen kilometres to the mono-port in DN 2 and Nan wants us to complete the distance in three hours.

That's doable. We are fit. Noah has encouraged us to use the gym and we have, but Nan, the tri-athlete, is fitter than I and has to pause for me to catch up a couple of times.

"You Admin bods are totally soft," she says to me the second time she waits. "We'll have to get you out on the farms when we get back."

"Is the heavy work not done by 'bots?" I ask. I know Tadz said they had to go back to basics, but surely the heaviest mauling is done by robots.

"No more. We lost some to the "Setback" and used others for parts. Plus, they need recharging all the time. We can't waste electricity; we have enough of a problem making it in the first place.'

We don't waste much breath talking but jog on towards our goal. Nan is expecting to use the mono-pod to take us to DN 1 when we arrive in DN 2, as she thinks we'll look less conspicuous that way. It makes me nervous, but I go along with it.

According to our TPs, it's five-twenty-four local time when we arrive. Nan is happy with that and we quickly change and slide as nonchalantly as we can onto the platform waiting for a cohort of cleaning robots to march past in order to hide among them. There is little dead time in the colony and there's always someone about, so we shouldn't be too obvious.

The eight and a half kilometers to the DN 1 mono-port in the centre of the dome seems endless. There are few people in the carriage this early in the morning, and I clasp my hands between my knees so that they cannot be seen shaking. Nan is so laid back she's examining her nails and making idle conversation with a young man seated across from her. I hardly think I can stand as the pod shudders to a halt in the port, but Nan is up and off with a cheery wave to her new friend.

Head high, she walks into the Administration building as if she has every right, which is, I know, the way to do it, but I'm still scared. I know where the PDB mainframe is, but access is restricted to all but a few. Nan slows and walks beside me as I make my way to the heart of the building. The mainframe is below, shielded from all. Normally, access is by the exclusive lift, but I do know there are stairs — in case. Nan stops by the lift.

"We can't use that. We need a fingerprint," I whisper.

Nan sighs, "Where are the stairs?"

I turn and head towards the door leading to them. I expect it to be locked but it isn't, and I can hear the whir of the cleaning robots at work. My mood lightens. We are here at exactly the right time, while the cleaners are busy. They are basic robots who cannot differentiate between specific humans. All locks will be off until they are finished. But, more importantly, all Controllers will stay out of the way. Unless there's an emergency everyone stays out of the way of the cleaning 'bots.

We hurry on down to the mainframe. This door is locked but Nan inputs the keycode without mishap and it glides open with the faintest puff of hydraulics. We are in.

I stand and stare. It is so big. I don't know why but I hadn't realised that it would be so big. I mean, it runs the whole colony, so I suppose it should be. It takes up the whole room, its banks forming corridors of intricate workings. I don't know what to do, but Nan is hurrying through with purpose.

She stops and turns to me, "Okay, where do I go?'

"Why ask me? It was your idea to come."

"I thought you worked with data?"

"I do, but I have my own console on the floor above. Only the exulted few ever come in here."

"Phuddle! Look for a keypad and be quick. We need to hurry."

"There'll be more than one keypad," I tell her.

"Yes, but there'll be the right one," she sniffs as if I was a number short of a keycode.

So, easy then, I think to myself, hoping I would recognise *the* keypad when I saw it. But I don't need telling twice, and we scuttle around inside the mainframe like frenzied minibots looking for problems to solve.

Suddenly I hear a squeak from the other side of the room. "Here Jax!" By the time I find Nan she has inserted a memory strip and is frantically tapping the icons on a vertical keypad. "Keep watch," she hisses.

Her fingers tap at the frame in impatience as the material she wants is downloaded. I am shaking again. I expect to hear sirens when she opens the programme she wants, but nothing changes. Is there a red light flashing somewhere, silently warning Control of our presence? I keep thinking I hear footsteps, but I'm imagining it … until suddenly I'm not.

I hear the soft sigh of the hydraulics and the swish of material rubbing against itself. Nan stops tapping and holds her hand for the machine to spit out the strip. Nothing happens. The swishing is moving in our direction. I am ready to run but Nan grabs my arm with one hand while still holding her other out for the strip.

I am about to pull away when the strip appears and she grabs it, slides it into a pocket and directs me to the far side of the room, away from the footsteps. We creep around the edge of the mainframe and make towards the door. We have to get out without raising suspicion. Nan indicates I should stand out of sight as she creeps towards the door and begins to enter the code. She holds one hand in the air as she taps and on the last number her hand drops, indicating I should join her. As I feared the sound of the hydraulics is noticed by whoever has entered.

"Hello? Is that you Controller Gil?"

I would have frozen, but Nan drags me through the door and races up the stairs, two at a time. We stop at the top and Nan peers around. We don't appear to have been followed. There is no one about, just a cleaner robot heading towards the exit. We need to get going before the door locks behind it. We fall in behind the machine and try to calm ourselves before leaving the building.

"Stop!" The tone invites no argument. We stop and turn. A Controller I do not recognise is standing behind us, flanked by two of the Security Team. She waits for us to approach her. "Why are you here at this time?" Her expression does not change.

I wait for Nan to speak. We have no way of knowing how much she knows.

"Well. I'm waiting."

"I asked them to meet me here." A new voice.

We both remain staring ahead hardly daring to breathe. I sense a figure move up from behind and stand by Nan.

"I was not informed."

"It was a last-minute thing. There's been a glitch with the data inputting process, and I asked if these two would drop everything and help. We don't want to make a drama out of a crisis, now, do we?"

"The Controller takes a deep breath before answering. "No, I suppose we don't." She spins on her heels and goes back the way she had come, with the two Security officers following.

"Quickly, girls. Out before she realises she's been tricked." Our saviour heads for the door expecting us to follow.

"Libby?" Nan queries in a hushed voice.

"Controller Libbette when you speak to me," Libby barks but we see her smile as she says it. She marches us to the mono-port. "Get on the first pod and get out of here. They'll soon suss the deception, and the Security Team are already on alert and out looking for anything suspicious. Stay watchful at all times."

"Will you be safe?" I ask. She's put herself in danger helping us.

"Don't worry about me. I have a story. Get out, now."

I open my mouth to tell her Braithe is worried about her, but she seems to melt into the growing crowd as people begin turning up for work.

"We'll be going the opposite way to the crowd," I suggest to Nan. "Do you think we'll be safe?"

Nan grabs my arm. "No. Look there's Security all over the port. This way."

We can't even get inside the port; there are members of the Security Team standing by the entrance both inside and out. They look mean and ready for business. We should have known the PDB would have a warning device within its system.

The crowd is thinning, not that it was ever very big in the first place. Nan seems to know where she is going, and I blindly follow.

She takes me away from the port and towards the Recreational Building. There are Security 'bots outside, but she veers to the right of the building, crouching slightly so the hedge around it conceals us. I have always marveled at the aesthetic touches in DN 1; now I'm thankful. The hedge is quite spindly at the back of the building, as if it doesn't matter where it can't be seen. Nan pushes through and I follow. She is standing by an inspection cover when I join her.

"Help me with this," she mutters quietly.

"That's the sewer." I hang back.

"Not just the sewer. There's cables and water pipes and inspection tunnels. Now help."

We drag the cover from over the chamber and slide down into the darkness. Nan, with my help, drags the cover back in place. I switch on my TP to give us some light and find that Nan is right. There is a sewer but there's also a tunnel which is dry and relatively clean for the technicians to inspect the pipes and cables that snake under the dome, supplying the living quarters and offices with water and energy. The tunnel is quite narrow but there's enough room for us in single file.

"'Bots are expensive and difficult to replace in colonies like this. They are not always used in sewers unless it's an emergency," Nan informs me as she studies her TP. I suddenly realize that this is BJ's domain. Nan reminds me of our situation as she points out, "This way."

"How do you know?"

"I have a plan of the underground tunnels. Remember I'm not one of you." She sets off at a cracking rate for someone nearly bent double, and I can only follow.

The way seems endless, and I frequently ask for rests, but Nan is insistent that we hurry along. Eventually she comes to a halt, and as I peer over her shoulder, I see the end of the tunnel.

"We should be at the mono-port and just need to go up," Nan says. She checks her TP and casts around in the ceiling of the tunnel. "There!" She nearly knocks me over as she turns to show me the underside of a narrow inspection cover, much smaller than the previous one.

"Do you think it's guarded?" I ask.

"Of course," she replies.

"Then what do we do?"

"Create a diversion," she tells me nonchalantly.

"How?"

I step back as she looks up, her face a hideous rictus in the eerie light from the TP in the ghostly darkness of the chamber. She turns and puts her shoulder under the cover, slowly lifting and peering out. She lets it drop and turns to me. "The guard is facing into the port. We'll emerge behind it. This chamber is fairly close to the tunnel door." She taps the TP, "Just as I'd hoped." She looks at me. "All you need to do is get into the tunnel and run like a Beast is after you until you reach our dome. Never mind about me." I can only stare at her. "I shall create the diversion and follow. Trust me. I've been in trickier spots before."

I'm about to object, but knowing Nan as I do, I nod reluctantly. She turns back to the cover.

Quietly and carefully, Nan lifts the cover and slides it far enough for me to emerge. Once I'm out she pushes with all her might and the cover glides like a curling stone across the polished floor, sweeping the feet from under the guard as it does so. In its panic, the gun it's carrying fires into the port, chipping cladding from the walls and sending the few people there scattering like so many insects.

I stand mesmerized but Nan is frantically waving her arm indicating I go.

I go. I get inside the tunnel and run like a Beast is after me, until I get a stitch in my side and double up against the wall. I'm not there long before Nan catches up with me, grinning from ear to ear.

"That was fun." She is breathless but pulls me forward. "We'll not be safe until we're in the Industrial Dome."

W E HAVE BEEN MISSED and Noah is waiting for us when we finally arrive back in the Agricultural Dome. He is not pleased.

"What the hell do you think you were doing?" He doesn't shout, but his voice is cold and hard. "You may have put everything we've worked for in jeopardy."

Nan rummages in her pocket and holds out the strip.

"What's this?" he snaps as he snatches it from her hand.

"All the data you said we need in order to launch an offensive," she tells him quietly. "Numbers, dates, designations." She bows her head and waits.

Noah turns the strip over and over and then turns on his heel and heads towards his office, "Come!" he snarls over his shoulder. We go.

We are filthy, tired, hungry, and thirsty, probably in that order but neither of us dare say anything to Noah. Braithe joins us but doesn't say anything either, and we avoid eye contact.

Noah inserts the strip into the computer and waits for the information. He and Braithe stare at the screen as he taps icons which take them through the data. Eventually he swings the seat round and looks at us. "Go and shower, get some supper and go to bed." His voice softens a little. "You both look all in. I'll be calling a meeting tomorrow and I need you to be alert."

As we turn to go, I look at Braithe. "We met Libby. She helped us. She's well."

"I hope, for your sake, she still is," Braithe says coldly.

Nan is uncharacteristically quiet as we shower and dress in borrowed bathrobes and make our way to our rooms with plates of unappetizing looking sandwiches. It is late and we meet no one. I'm very tired but too restless to sleep. I should have realised that we would compromise Libby and that thought keeps me awake long into the night.

Breakfast is a subdued affair. There is tea and some pancakes which are heavy and chewy. The new cook has a face that is just as heavy and as sour as the syrups he produces. I know she did wrong, but I still miss Janet, with her bustle and light pastries. There is no sign of Noah or Braithe, and Attercliffe is noticeable by his absence.

There is no automated disposal here, so we help wash up for something to do. When we have finished, we make our way down to the Beasts and the comfort of Nan's dad. He's just as cross with us for putting Libby in danger, so we go to the orchard, where we hide until the lunchtime crowd has finished. It is late into the afternoon by the time we feel comfortable enough to go to the Refectory.

Noah is sitting in his usual spot at the table when we go in. I stop and hang back, but Nan goes to the counter and selects food from what is left before taking a seat at his table.

"Join me," Noah shoots a friendly look in my direction as he says this, so I quickly fill a plate and join him and Nan.

"The information you got is very important to us, but you cannot go off on your own like that."

"The end result is good though," says Nan with her mouth full.

"This time. But you could have been caught, and as it is, we won't know how Libby will fare. You will have most certainly compromised her position."

Nan puts down her fork. "I'm sorry. I didn't think."

"You rarely do. That's what makes you both a good and a bad operative. You're willing to take chances, but you can be over impulsive."

I am very concerned about Libby and feel responsible for her safety, so ask, "Do you think Libby will be alright?"

Noah's attitude suddenly changes. "Only time will tell," he says, without emotion. "There's a meeting tonight, after supper. With the information you have gathered, we can now plan an operation. Be there." He spits out the last two words, and the meal is finished in silence.

•   •   •

We creep into the back of the dining area that evening, as we don't know what people know of our exploits. By now, we are not feeling so blasé about what we have done.

Tadz beckons us over to his table. He isn't smiling but he clears a space for us to sit. Jared is sitting at the same table. There is a feeling of nervous expectation and the conversations around the room are muted.

Without warning Noah stands and the room goes quiet.

"Some vitally important data has been made available," Noah begins. A few pairs of eyes look in our direction, but as Noah doesn't name us, they eventually look away. "There is still some heavily coded information within the files which will take time to decipher. However, I have been in a meeting with The Caputa all morning and she has decided that there is enough information to begin an offensive."

A murmur washes around the room, soft as the summer breeze in my dome.

He raises his hand for silence. "It needs to be planned meticulously, as I doubt there will be second chances. I have forwarded a summary of what The Caputa and I have learnt from the information strip to your TP's. Please read it and consider strategies. I will be here for the next few hours should you wish to converse face to face. Otherwise, forward your ideas via your TP."

Tadz has been busy reading the findings throughout Noah's speech. Nan and I skim the pages, but Jared appears disinterested and continues to eat, returning to the counter to sweep up any leftovers.

"It lookz like we could do an awful lot via the computer zystem," Tadz tells us. "If we could re-programme all the 'botz to our zide, we've already won. There doezn't zeem to be many zapient beingz who are likely to be a problem."

"How so?" asks Nan.

"There are a lot of workers." I tell them.

"The workerz are half doped on Midazolam; they won't know what'z hit them. They'll just follow routine regardlezz of leadership," Tadz remarks. I hadn't thought of that. "The Controllerz have drugged them to make them eazy to control. It workz both wayz. There are very few actual Controllerz. They rely on the 'botz and for the drugged workerz to toe the line. That name ..." he jabs his finger onto the screen. "I know that name from zomewhere." He points to the leader of the Controllers. "It'll come to me, I'm sure." He taps away at the TP and sits back with satisfaction, looking towards Noah as if waiting for a reaction. It doesn't take long.

"Tadz." Noah gets to his feet. "This is sound but for one thing." Tadz remains seated and smiling. "We would need Libby to carry it out. She knows the computer network inside out, but we don't know her position at the moment. We can't rely on her and there's no one else with that sort of knowledge."

"There iz," says Tadz. "Jared."

Jared's head shoots up. "Heh?"

"Who?" Noah appears mystified.

"Jared, your brother." Tadz reminds him.

Noah clearly has no idea what his brother can or cannot do, and the look on Jared's face just confirms it. I begin to feel sorry for the sullen teenager.

"Jared has excellent programming skillz. I know the lazy little servbot hidez his skillz and moztly usez them for gaming, but he haz helped me enormouzly by building programmez into my zyztem to further the ztudy of the creaturez." Tadz then delivers his piece de resistance. "He haz alzo hacked into the zyztem in the Admin Domez to keep track of Libby for me."

"Why haven't you told me?" Braithe is on her feet.

"You didn't azk, my dear," replies Tadz coolly.

I look from one to the other. All is not well in the dome, I feel.

"So we needn't have gone to DN 1?" cries Nan.

"Well, zertain filez are better protected than otherz. Alzo, we don't know if they were on to uz or not. At leazt we know we have all the information now and that it'z good ztuff. Not zomething put out for uz to find." Tadz pats her hand in a patronising manner.

"What about Libby?" Braithe asks with concern. You can hear the tremble in her voice.

"She'z gone quiet. Zorry." Tadz doesn't sound sorry. He stands in the silence and looks towards Noah. 'Shall we go ahead?"

•　　•　　•

I have so many questions, and fire them at Nan as soon as we are alone. "What was that all about? Did you know about Jared's skills? Do you know something about Libby? Does your dad know?"

"For goodness sake, Jax, slow down. One at a time, please."

But she then goes on to answer them all, just not in any particular order.

"Libby is okay. Dad just wants the pair of them to sweat a bit. She's not brilliant, but okay. She's sent a message. We have a code; Jared devised it. She wants to stay and is in hiding until they forget her ..."

"But they ..."

"Don't worry. Jared has sent that message to her. She probably knows they don't forget anyway; she's been there a while. She'll find a way out. Now, as to "what was that all about?" Dad has never liked the way Noah treats his brother and has told him so. Jared is very intelligent but has always been pushed into the background by his big brother. Noah's so up himself that it developed into an argument which has not been settled, so they needle each other whenever they get the opportunity. Braithe's no better."

"She's always been fine with me," I retort. I'm finding this in-fighting a tad unnerving. Haven't we got enough on our plates without resorting to internal arguments?

"Have you crossed her yet?"

"Well, no, but ..."

"Wait 'til you do, then you'll find out. And — what was it? Oh, yes. Yes, I do know about Jared, obviously, but as Noah doesn't really care, it has become shared knowledge between ourselves. He thinks Libby does all the network stuff on her own. He doesn't realize that she and Jared are working together."

"Doesn't Jared care?" I do, for him.

"No, not really. There's no love lost there. It started after the "Setback." Jared was only little. His mother was dead and his father was working all hours and he didn't understand. Noah didn't handle it very well."

I couldn't remember my family and didn't know how to respond, so moved on. "What do we do now?"

"Nothing. That's the hardest part," sighs Nan. "We can only wait and see."

Tadz had pushed Jared towards Noah's office and they had disappeared inside and firmly closed the doors, so Nan and I make our way to my room, where we idle the time away eating biscuits and drinking home-made fruit juice until we fall asleep.

•   •   •

We are abruptly rocketed from deep sleep to wakefulness by Nils banging on the door shouting, "Call to Arms! Call to Arms!"

"What the bloody hell? Nils ... pack it in," grumbles Nan as she opens the door.

"What's to do, Nils?" I ask.

"Jared's finished," Nils informs us, "and Noah's calling everyone to the Refectory. It doesn't matter what you're supposed to be doing. This is more important." With that, he runs down the corridor towards the stairs as if fearful of missing something.

We are not the first in the dining room, but nor are we the last, so sit kicking our heels waiting for everyone to arrive. It is very early morning. We must have slept through the night. I am hungry but there is no breakfast. I don't know if I should have been expecting some.

Jared looks different; he looks important. He is sitting straight-backed at the front of the group. He has his brother on his right and Tadz on his left. He has washed and braided his hair and is wearing a clean uniform which looks new.

Noah opens the meeting. "I have called you here to apprise you of what Jared has discovered on the data strip brought back from the Admin Domes. He has worked through the night, and we now are fully aware of the situation. It is ..." he pauses and looks around. "It is both better and worse than we thought. The Controllers have made Dome 1 their own little sanctuary, with small agricultural plots cared for by robots. Officially there are only twenty-five Controllers, but this number has grown as family members have been included. At the present time, there are eighty-three personnel enjoying perks we can only dream of."

"We can muster more than that, can't we?" someone calls from the centre of the room.

"Barely, but yes we can. On top of that, Jared has reprogrammed all 'bots in such a way that, should the Controllers be attacked, the robots will not support them but join the side of the attackers. Anyway, some of the privileged will be minors, and in no way are we to hurt them. In fact, we don't want to hurt anyone ..."

"Come on Noah — they eat people!" someone shouts.

"Aye, they live a life of luxury on the backs of slaves."

Braithe raps the table, and the noise quietens, although there's still murmurings.

"We are not like them. We mustn't sink to their level," Noah warns. "We want to stop this, not create a new dictatorship. Just because I say we shouldn't hurt them does not mean they will not receive sanctions."

"I don't think everyone agrees with him," whispers Nan, looking around. "In fact, most people look ready for war."

"Bloody hell, Nan ..." I grab her arm. Jared is standing and there is instant silence.

"There is one thing Noah hasn't told you," Jared states. "The person behind all this is Branchard."

Nan cringes as if all hell is about to break loose, but there is, for a moment, a stunned silence. Then all hell does break loose. People are on their feet, shouting and swearing. I hear the muted bang as a cup is thrown across the room. Fists are raised and a few have stormed out of the building in a hurry.

"Who is this Branchard?" I gasp.

"Don't ask," Nan snaps irritably, her face morphing. I now see what I didn't see the first time in the tunnels—the snake beneath the human façade.

I turn away. This is taking a scary turn.

Jared sits down quietly and remains perfectly still, a sly smile on his face. He makes no attempt to quell the crowd, but eventually Braithe manages to make herself heard over the noise and calls for quiet and for one question at a time.

A voice in the crowd asks, "Does The Caputa know about this? What does she say?"

Noah rises to his feet. "Yes she does. I spoke to her as soon as I had all the details. I told her that Branchard was behind it all, and it was she who insists that no one is hurt. She does want Branchard — for herself."

The tone is ominous but does nothing to placate the crowd. I wonder again who this Branchard is, and what he has done to cause such a furor.

The crowd are angry, and nothing Braithe or Noah say goes any way to stopping them. They are on their feet, shouting and pushing. Only Tadz and Jared are seated; Tadz stone-faced, Jared still with the sly smile on his. Nan grabs my arm and pulls me to the back of the room and the door to outside.

We normally head for the orchard to chat, but Nan takes me to the back of the tower, and we watch as the others stream out and towards their own apartments and farms.

"What's going on? Where are they going? Should we follow them? Who's Branchard?" I ask fearfully.

"We are staying here. They'll be back."

"Who is Branchard, Nan?"

"The Caputa's brother. In a nutshell — Branchard thought he should be President of the Federation. The presidency is not a given right; it needs to be earned, and by the peoples' vote. Branchard is not a very nice being."

I snort, "That sounds like an understatement."

"Anyway, there's been a feud between them for ages now, and most people here blame them both for the 'Setback', whether they were involved or not. Feelings will be high, and I fear some will take proceedings into their own hands."

"Has your dad anything to do with this?"

"Probably."

"You don't seem too concerned," I snap at her.

"We've been too long caught up in the fight between them. The whole situation is a pustule that needs lancing. Perhaps we can build on the remains. Build something better." Nan sighs.

"What about Noah?"

"What about him? He's too soft to make a real difference. He'd let Branchard get away if left to his own devices."

"What about Libby?" I whisper.

"Libby's made of sterner stuff. She runs the Resistance, although Noah likes to think he does."

We watch and wait in silence until Nan's superior hearing picks something up. "Shh! I think they're coming back."

The people of the dome are beginning to return, carrying all manner of farming tools and sharp looking implements. That they are angry shows on their faces and in the purposeful pace in which they march past us and towards the tunnel.

"Surely you're not going with them?" I demand of Nan as she rises.

"Try and stop me. I wouldn't miss this for the world."

THEY HAVE GATHERED at the edge of the dome, and there's a blockage at the mouth of the tunnel, the seething crowd waiting impatiently, muttering and shuffling.

"Are we waiting for Jared?" I ask. "Is this what he was planning? Is he going to lead?"

"Jared will lead from the rear with Tadz," Nan explains. "He'll man the computer and direct the groups to the best advantages. He'll not get his hands dirty. Nor will my father. Wind-up merchants, they are."

"Is that what you think of them?" I'm aghast that there seems to be no familial affection.

"I mean that in the best way. The crowd needs winding up, especially Noah. Braithe will lead with Grainne Phillips, and Libby, hopefully, on the inside."

That comment sparks a thought. "What about Romney?"

"Romney will do what Romney will do. We can't trust her."

"What about Noah? Won't he be coming?"

"I doubt it. He'll coordinate things from this end, liaising with Tadz and Jared in order to influence the two factions."

"You seem to know a lot about it," I mutter crossly. In truth, I feel a tad sidelined.

"I've known them for a lot longer than you. I know how they work. There's plenty of us going through, and if Jared's done his job properly, it should be all over quite quickly. Then Noah will sweep in then and take the credit." Nan sounds very cynical.

"That doesn't sound very kind," I snap.

"But the truth, I suspect."

Our arguing is brought to a halt as Braithe appears, with Grainne Phillips, the gentle farmer's wife I met the other day, at her side. She doesn't look so gentle now. Both are wearing leather jackets, and Grainne's boys bring a barrow full of similar items for the crowd. A number of people look askance and stare at Braithe.

Braithe interprets the stares correctly and explains, "As you know, most of those we will come against will be 'bots, and they should be compromised, but we're taking no chances. Not all the Security Team are robots, so we are hoping that these will stop the stun effect of any of their weapons, should it come to that." She looks around at the expectant faces. "Okay, if we're all here, I'll explain the plan."

There are nods of acknowledgement and Braithe and Grainne move to a position in front of the tunnel.

"We go at a walking pace through the tunnels ..."

"Why? Why not hurry through and get this over with," calls a voice from the centre of the crowd.

"If we lose control we are lost," Braithe insists. "We have to look like a professional fighting unit — not a rabble. Although, I'm hoping this will be over without much of a fight."

"What's the point in us going, then?" the same voice calls and a murmur of agreement swirls around him. An electronic saw is raised from somewhere within the group.

"We need to round up the Controllers. We don't want innocents — regardless of who they are — to be hurt. This is about stopping abuse, not starting our own," Grainne warns the crowd.

"But ..."

Braithe stops the voice with a sharp retort. "This is wasting time. Fall in behind Grainne and myself. Remain there through the tunnels and follow our lead when we reach the first inhabited dome. We expect most of the Controllers to be in DN 1, which is the second habited dome we will reach. I repeat, we want no innocent bystanders injured. It won't help our cause."

Despite a low growl of murmurings, the crowd form an untidy rabble behind Braithe and Grainne. I am not convinced any good is going to come from it.

Nan is pushing her way into the crowd, but I pull her back. "What's the matter now, Jax?" she sighs.

"Look at them. Just stand back and look, Nan. This isn't going to end well, and I don't want to be in the middle of it." To her credit, Nan does as I suggest. "There's a group in the centre who look too militant." I point them out. "If they decide to take matters into their own hands, the advantage will be lost. If we stand back, we might be able to do something about them." Nan doesn't say anything. "Lead from the rear," I urge.

"You might be right," she considers. "Okay, we'll do that. Grainne and Braithe at the head and us at the tail."

I'm not convinced that she has taken my point, but don't feel I can insist any further.

•   •   •

Braithe's idea of walking pace is not quite the same as mine, and we jog through the tunnel to the ruined domes. The ordered column begins to disintegrate once in the first of the wrecked Industrial sites, and a few of the noisy individuals try to move past the two leaders. They are soon pushed back when Grainne suggests we all stop and wait until everyone is following orders and back in line. The fear of contamination is strong, and no one wants to be amongst the dust and corruption for any longer than necessary.

Nan nudges my arm. "I see that narky group have managed to stay at the front this time," she whispers. "I think you're right about there being trouble." They are all carrying tools of one sort or another and all look like they could inflict some damage.

The cracking pace continues, and we reach DN 2 in a little under three hours. Being at the back of the line, I only realise that we have reached the dome by the shout that goes up as the door is breached. By the time Nan and I reach the exit, the crowd have scattered through the streets and are wreaking havoc among the normal residents.

We see weapons raised in threats to the local people who just stand around looking scared. Some have been taken captive for whatever reason. It's not them we have the grievance with. We can see Braithe and Grainne racing away from them. They are not trying to stop the mob, and for a minute I wonder if I have missed something — been left out of the planning for some reason.

I then realize that it would have been impossible for just the two of them to stop so many, and they were heading for DN 1 in the hope that they could reach it before being captured.

"We'll follow Braithe and Grainne," Nan announces, and we take advantage of the mayhem to slide through and head towards the other side of the dome.

They are some distance ahead, but we know where they're heading and set off in that direction. No one takes any notice of us; everyone from the Admin Dome looks confused and seem to be running around aimlessly, while those from the Agricultural Dome try to round them up with whatever force they deem necessary.

"It's like herding rabbits," Nan mutters as we push on.

I've never considered the idea of herding rabbits but from my limited knowledge of the creatures I think I know what she means. Rabbits are timid and hopeless in a crisis.

I've watched them in the petting zoo. They just scatter when the keeper goes in to pick one up for us to hold in the hope that it catches one of the others.

I also seem to remember from my history sessions that ancient people used to eat them. We are all just rabbits.

THERE IS MAYHEM all around me. The people from the Agricultural Domes are forcing the residents of the Admin Domes into the towers. They are not being gentle about it either, even though there is no resistance. I am horrified at the escalation of the violence. It's not the workers we have come to tackle. They are the victims in all of this, and I thought the idea was to free them of their drugged slavery and stop the euthanasia and processing of human flesh.

My breath sticks in my throat, and I have to stop, but Nan races on, seemingly oblivious of the mayhem around her. Many people from the Agricultural Domes have gone berserk, letting out the pent-up anger they have against the Administrators. They don't seem to care what they do to others. I have no wish to be caught on my own and make ready to follow, but in that brief moment I lose sight of Nan, although not for long.

As I make ready to sprint after her, I see her fall. It takes forever and no time at all. Her legs are swept from under her, and she falls heavily. As she tries to get up, the person who had felled her clubs her around the head with a shovel and she falls back. My vision tunnels and I make to go to her aid, but two things stop me. The first is a vice-like hand on my shoulder. The second is when the realisation hits me that the person attacking her is one of our own. Those from the Admin Domes are scuttling away from any confrontation in panic. I try to pull away from the hand and go to my friend, but it is too strong and the moment is lost.

"There's nothing you can do."

I recognise the voice.

"Romney?"

Her hand falls away and I turn to face her.

"Glutton for punishment are we?" She is grinning in a very uncomfortable way. "What do you want this time?"

I know I'm not thinking as I say, "I'm looking for Branchard."

I don't know why I say it. I suppose it makes some sort of sense, as I am so angry over Nan's attack. Nan, my friend, despite her acerbic attitude and cutting remarks, is the only one I can talk to who understands what it is like in the Admin Domes.

I'd been told we can't trust Romney, but I feel confident that she would know how to reach Branchard, and in this moment I want to look him in the eye and, in the absence of a sharp stick, spit in it.

She looks at me, and for a moment I feel I see the true Romney beneath the hard exterior. Then her gaunt hand grasps my wrist, and she pulls me away from the mono-port that would take us to DN1.

"Where are we going?" I manage to gasp as distrust rises to the surface.

"You want to see Branchard? Come with me."

"Are you sure this is the right way?" I expect that he is in DN1 where all the business takes place. I'm concerned that she is taking me to Security Enforcement, and I'll never see not only Branchard, but anyone else I know, again.

She just sighs and shakes her head as she drags me on.

Romney heads for the park. There is a café there and it appears that is where we are heading. Apart from a few people standing about looking bewildered, the park is empty, as most of the dome's inhabitants are standing about elsewhere looking bewildered. How did we come to this?

Romney takes me to the back of the café, which is overshadowed by trees. I see a tubular pod attached to the back of the kitchen. I'd not noticed it before, and I pass by on a regular basis, but as it is obscured by the branches of the trees, perhaps I can be forgiven. Romney places her hand flat against the keypad and a door glides open without so much as a whisper from the mechanism. She pushes me inside, and for a moment I panic and turn and grab at her wrist.

"It's okay, I'm coming," she mumbles and steps in beside me.

My heart is banging in my chest and my vision has tunneled at the thought that she might have been sending me alone to my doom.

"Hold tight," she tells me as the door shuts behind her.

We are in an elevator, with pristine white walls padded in a soft material and plenty of room for the two of us. There is no keypad with floor numbers and no apparent means of starting the lift, but I know we are falling. There is nothing with which to gauge the rate of descent, but it seems to go on for a long time. The stop is so smooth I'm not prepared for the opening of the door.

"Glory be, but you are terrified," Romney says as she stares at me. "What will you do when you meet Branchard?"

With that, she starts to laugh, and it's not a pleasant sound. Now that time has passed I'm not so sure I should be looking for the enemy in his lair, but there's nothing I can do about it.

THE CORRIDOR SEEMS ENDLESS. There are numerous turns, and I suspect that it spreads underneath both of the Admin Domes and probably even the complex. I do know I shall never be able to find my own way back. I guess we are heading towards the underside of DN 1, but I wouldn't stake my life on it.

Eventually we come to the end of the tunnel, and Romney stops and turns to look closely at me. "We're here. Follow my lead and all will be well. Just don't listen to *him*." She sounds different, calm and in control, and then she changes again back to the woman I had met earlier. "I don't know what you're expecting but I doubt he'll comply."

With that, she places her hand onto an all-but invisible keypad and a door silently glides open in the wall before me. Romney steps inside and indicates I follow.

I hadn't really given any thought as to what to expect. I suppose something akin to The Caputa and her lair. This isn't even close. It is sumptuous to the point of insult. The room is large, spacious and perfectly arranged, with extravagant murals on the walls, comfortable seating, ankle-deep carpet and tables set with types of food and drink I have never seen or smelt in my entire life. That is, if my memory had been working at full capacity during my previous life, which I doubt.

Movement catches my peripheral vision and I turn in time to see a gorgeously dressed creature rise from one of the cushion-strewn banquettes.

At first I think it's The Caputa, but then realized that this Arak is not as tall as I remember The Caputa to be and is considerably slighter. The hair is the same multi-colour, long and braided, but the skin tones lighter. The eyes are the same startling blue, and they are watching for my reaction. I feel he knows all about me.

"So you're one of the little earthlings set on entering my realm." The voice is soft and beguiling, I could listen to it all day. "Come sit and tell all."

He indicates that I should take the seat he has just vacated. I don't move, and he laughs. He turns to Romney and orders her to provide refreshment for me, flashing her a brilliant smile, but she doesn't move either.

"Come Romney, she'll need sustenance sometime." The voice is harder this time.

I keep Romney in my peripheral vision. She is moving slowly, taking her time choosing. My mind goes back to the food I took for testing. Surely this isn't drugged? I could see Branchard eating us, but he wouldn't want to eat drugged food — but then, he isn't eating.

Suddenly I have a thought. It feels like an explosion within me, and I am convinced that Branchard can see my thoughts. He knew we were coming, that *I* was coming. He knows everything.

My mouth is dry, but I manage to say, "Who told?" It comes out like a squeak, but he hears and bursts out laughing.

"My, my but you're far too clever for the other side. Put that down, Romney, and fetch something more wholesome. I want to chat to this young lady properly."

He watches her leave before throwing himself down onto one of the heavily cushioned couches. He waits until the door closes before turning his gaze to me and again indicates that I join him.

I don't want to but feel compelled to sit. My legs seem to lose their use and I drop into a chair opposite where he is sitting. I know he is watching me, but I refuse to raise my head and give him eye contact.

"I'd like you to meet someone." He bends forward and I instinctively flinch, which makes him laugh again. He is a very handsome man, but I feel no attraction, only fear.

The door through which Romney left slides open, and I am expecting her to walk through with the food, but it's not her. I feel my breath stick in my throat, and I am sure I am going to pass out as the colour fades from the world around me.

"I thought you'd be surprised," he murmurs, as Libby takes a seat beside him. "Meet the wife, as you humans say." He puts one of his many arms around her shoulder and pulls her against him.

The smell of the food around me is filling my head and making me gag. I think I might be sick. I have felt an affinity with Libby for so long that the shock of finding her to be in league with Branchard is like falling from a very high building. My stomach is convulsing and my head spinning.

"Your little friend doesn't look too well," says the velvet voice that I am beginning to hate. "Perhaps we'd better prepare a room for her. We can chat when she feels better."

I look towards Libby, although I can hardly bring myself to give her eye contact. Branchard's arm is still draped over her shoulder and she is leaning towards him. I am repulsed and feel the need to attack her.

"But they killed Sanderson. Sanderson, your son. My friend," I spit at her.

Her cheeks glow with red spots as she looks at me.

"There must be some sacrifice for The Cause," she whispers.

"Oh, I can assure you we didn't," the oily voice breaks in. "That was a complete accident. Although, to be fair, he did deserve it."

I just want to get away from them both. How Libby can stand by and allow that to happen to her son and carry on as if nothing has changed, I do not know. How can she let that oily creep paw her?

Romney must have returned, although I hadn't noticed her. She is now told to take me somewhere, and to be honest I've given up caring what happens to me. She guides me to what turns out to be a comfortable guest room. She lets me in and then places the tray she is carrying on the table.

"It's okay," she tells me in a hushed whisper. "There're no additives and it's proper food — Controller food." I don't react, as I'm not surprised she knows about the food. "Just keep your head down. This is between Branchard and Cazeta. We're just in the wrong place at the wrong time."

"Who on Ceres is Cazeta?" I demand.

"You know her as The Caputa. Branchard's sister. They're at war and we're the collateral. Try and get some rest — and eat something. You'll need to keep your strength up if you're going to get out of here."

•　　　•　　　•

I know I need rest and food, but that's easier said than done. I pace for a while. Then I try one of the sandwiches, which only makes me realise how hungry I actually am, so I eat the lot and drink the tea, although it isn't very nice as I've let it go cold. I lay down and toss and turn for a while. I must have fallen asleep because I suddenly find myself being woken by Romney.

"If we're going to do something about the Branchard/Cazeta situation you'd better come with me now," she growls in my ear.

"Why now?" I ask between gulps of the drink she's brought me.

"Libby's drugged him. He's fast asleep."

"Libby? But I thought ..."

"I know what you thought, but she's been working undercover for so long now she can play the game better than anyone."

"How did she cope when Sanderson died?"

"Don't ask. You nearly undid her when you questioned her feelings for him, but she's good. By glory, she's good." Romney was looking around the door and into the corridor.

"What happens now?"

"We're taking him to the PolliPauz while there's confusion above ground." She beckons me out.

"Who's taking him where?" I fall in beside her.

"I found Grainne and Braithe, and with your help we are taking him to PolliPauz on the other side of the planet. With a bit of luck, Noah, Tadz and Jared will have got The Caputa there. It's an Arak fight. Let them fight away from us."

"Has this always been the plan? I thought we were hiding The Caputa? Why wasn't everyone in on it? What's with ...?"

"So many questions. There's a spy in the camp, that much is certain — and not just Janet. Branchard knows too much. Libby going through a connubial ceremony with him means he doesn't feel the need to check the information he is being fed. So he got false information — well not exactly false but not entirely correct either."

Some things are beginning to make sense now. I had been introduced to The Caputa as if she was the be all and end all, but Noah and Janet weren't so impressed with her.

"But people have been hurt. Nan has been killed."

"Do you know that for sure?"

"Well no — not for sure. But she's been hurt and by someone from the Agricultural Dome."

"It all adds to the confusion," was the dry comment. "Come we need to get moving."

Romney hurries through the tunnels without faltering, and I am glad to follow. We emerge in Branchard's lair to find Libby and Braithe waiting for us. Libby has commandeered one of the re-programmed maintenance robots, who has Branchard awkwardly in his cart and covered with bedding.

"Where's Grainne?" Romney asks.

"Don't worry, she's just checking that the coast is clear," Libby tells her.

As soon as Grainne reappears and declares all is well, she, Romney and I set off with Branchard. Braithe stays with her sister, as they have other plans.

We head for the mono-port, walking openly through deserted streets. I wonder where everyone is, but dare not ask in case I don't like the answer. I wonder briefly how we would explain the trolley, as soiled bedding is sent down the laundry chute and not collected, but as there is no one about, it is irrelevant.

When I lived in the Admin Dome the mono-pods ran automatically every five minutes. There appears to be no break in the system, so we take the next one to DN 1, and from there we head towards the SpaceBus departure lounge as if we were catching the next ship to Mars.

Romney takes us to an unmarked door to the right of the main entrance. I had not been in the SpaceBus departure lounge before, so presumed it was something to do with maintenance, but inside was a spacious room containing space suits, oxygen cylinders and other essentials for a foray onto the surface of the planet.

I have never hankered to go out onto the surface of Ceres. It is extremely cold and inhospitable, and the darkness drops rapidly. You have to be properly suited, and the suits are bulky and cumbersome.

Needs must though, and I find myself being fitted into a spacesuit and helping the others into theirs. It is a struggle to get Branchard's lifeless form into one, but Romney is none too careful and makes no apologies for unceremoniously stuffing him in. Only the robot doesn't need any form of protection. As maintenance, it may have to leave the dome in order to carry out repairs, so is constructed accordingly.

Fortunately, the robot knows the procedure for opening the doors. I certainly don't, and nor do the others, it seems. We find ourselves standing in a large hangar which houses a number of all-terrain vehicles designed to stand up to the pressures of Ceres in the raw.

"Does anyone know how to drive one of these things?" I ask. I know of their existence, but this is the first time I have actually been up close and personal to one.

"The robot will," Romney says with confidence. "It will have to know how to get to where the trouble is so it can sort it out."

I sincerely hope she's right.

THE POLLIPAUZ IS NOTHING like I thought it would be, not that I'd given it a lot of thought. Things have been rather hectic.

First, I presume it is a building inside a dome. It is not, but then, it has not been designed with humans in mind. It is a solid round transparent structure built to withstand the rigors of the inhospitable planet, with external chambers allowing safe entrance or exit.

There is a building standing behind it and connected by a tunnel. It has some strange writing on it which is damaged in places. Romney tells me that it's the hotel, and the writing is Arak. The PolliPauz is damaged but not uninhabitable and I remember Nan explaining that some of the building had been used to make repairs to the domes.

"The safe entrance is this way," Grainne tells us through the communication system. We don't have far to go and are soon inside the safety chamber. "You should be able to remove your helmets once we get inside. Don't remove anything else, though. It's not safe."

We are the first there and wait impatiently for the others. I wander around the room we find ourselves in.

It is rather like a decrepit Travel-Exchange refreshment area, the sort of café you would find anywhere within the civilised Solar System. Not that I've ever been to one. I've only seen them in films that are set on other settled planets. There is a gaming area off to one side, and currency machines where you can check what credits you have to spend. It appears that we are not the only ones to use that system. There are tables and chairs arranged near the outside wall, giving a view of the lifeless lump of rock called Ceres, and a counter where you would be served. There's a square of a different colour where the credit terminal would have stood. It is dusty and strewn with discarded tableware and odd, dried stains that make me turn back to the others.

"Noah's taking his time," Romney observes.

"He's on his way. He has further to come than us," Grainne reminds her.

Romney wanders around the PolliPauz but every so often she stares through the walls looking for the others.

"Can you contact him?" Romney is whining to Grainne as I join the group.

"He'll be here," she snaps, but looks concerned all the same.

I see some movement through the walls of the PolliPauz. "Someone's coming now," I tell them.

Noah, Tadz and Jared have not been so thoughtful with The Caputa. She is bound and gagged and supported in a wheeled chair which bumps and clatters into the building just as Branchard begins to stir.

•　　　•　　　•

The siblings are sat facing each other with a table between. Noah leaves The Caputa tied where she is, but helps to move Branchard from the maintenance truck to a chair, where he is fastened. The gags are removed and Tadz provides some liquid in a flask, which both Araks ignore. The Caputa appears to have zoned out as if she has shut down and shut us out, but Branchard is glaring angrily about.

"Drink," Noah tells them as he sticks two straws into the flask. "It will help you to concentrate."

Both remain silent.

"Okay. Suit yourselves. The reason we have resorted to this is because we will not continue allowing you to treat human beings in the way you do."

Branchard glares at him, and for a moment I expect there to be some aggravation, but he just snorts loudly and a smirk slides across his face. "It's taken you long enough."

"You saw to that," Noah retorts, "by creating the 'Setback'. Our priority became the fight for survival against the elements. It is thanks to The Caputa ..."

"Fuck that!" sneers Branchard. "My beloved sister only helped you because she needed you — as well as a bit of comfort for herself."

"This, my friendz, is getting uz nowhere," Tadz breaks in.

"I say we set the Beasts on them and be done with," Jared snarls. "They'll blame each other, and we know neither is really on our side. So, let out the Beasts."

Both pale at the thought. Noah draws a deep breath and turns to his brother. "The Caputa is President of the UFP. You won't get away with her murder."

"What murder? It will be an accident involving the Beasts — won't it?" Jared's face has a look of utmost innocence. "Come on, Noah. You know we're just collateral. Well, the collateral is fighting back. And I mean fighting. No mealy-mouthed talks. That one ..." he pokes his index finger towards Branchard, "... will wheedle his way out of hell if it suits him."

"He'z right," Tadz interrupts. "He'z zilver-tongued. Isn't that what you say?"

Noah turns to The Caputa. "You're quiet. What have you to say?" Jared makes an exasperated noise and turns away.

"He's my brother," she says.

"You keep saying that, but you can't let him keep on doing what he's doing."

"You don't understand."

"Make me."

"You don't understand the nature of Arak siblings. If I report him to The Federation, he will be arrested, tried, condemned and terminated."

"And?" snaps Jared.

"If he dies, I die."

"How do you work that one out?" Jared is suspicious; I can tell by the tone of his voice.

"Arak mothers only give birth once — to a number of infants." The Caputa turns her head towards him. "The siblings share one essence from birth. If one is hurt, the others feel it. If one dies the others die. Fact."

Noah looks thoughtful. "Does he have to die? Life incarceration is another option surely?"

"Not with The Federation and not for his crimes," The Caputa informs him. "How many died in the 'Setback'? All were sapient beings. And how many have died since due to him?"

"But you are The President. Can't you have a say?"

"No one is above the Law. That's what makes it work. All sapient beings are equal and subject to the same laws and protections."

"So how has that worked for the people on Ceres?" Jared snarls. "They've had no protection from your vicious brother."

"I'm sorry. He's *my* brother."

"But the death penalty is hardly fair on Araks," I have to say. "You didn't cause the "Setback."" I look around the others before turning back to The Caputa. "Did you?" I ask her.

The Caputa turns to me and I shiver. "I didn't stop it. I knew what he was planning, what would occur, and I didn't stop it."

"How could you?" I want to know.

"As we experience each other's pain, so we know each other's thoughts. I could have warned the Federation."

"Would you have been able to without him knowing?" Grainne asks sharply.

The Caputa shrugs, "I don't know."

"I zuggezt you do but refuze to admit it," says Tadz. "I zuggezt you could and it would have been life imprizonment because the crime would have been intent, not murder." He turns away with an exasperated scoff.

"Your Presidency would not have survived his crime, would it?" Noah asks quietly. Dark red spots burn on The Caputa's cheeks. "Because what he does, you are capable of doing."

Jared snorts again, "She was feeding him information." Everyone turns to look at The Caputa. "If they share thoughts, then he would know what was being planned."

"She wasn't privy to everything," Noah told him. "I made sure of that."

"Couldn't you have talked to him?" I ask her naively.

"Not Branchard. He is evil through and through. It would have been death or nothing. If I had killed him, then I and my other siblings would have died. That's what stopped me."

"So, hundreds died instead," snarled Jared. "My mother. My father. Other parents. And more have died since, to feed your slaves."

"We are not cannibals," Grainne interjected. "It's abhorrent to us. You're cruel." A tear runs down her face and she makes no effort to wipe it away.

"Our fathers die after copulation and our mothers die as they give birth. We eat our dead. We have never experienced your sentimental upbringings," Branchard sneers. "We manage."

I step back as Jared looks ready to do him harm. He remembers and misses his family. I miss having family, strange as that sounds, and my memory is coming back. I understand, but want no part in the violence. It would make us as bad as them.

A noise stops the conversation, and we turn as one towards the safe entrance. The figure in the doorway stops and removes the helmet. It's Libby.

"Well, here we all are," she smiles.

THERE IS A SILENCE so deep it is tangible. The expressions of hope, mistrust and fear that cross not just one, but all the faces present, shows the level of perplexity in the room.

I wonder where Braithe is. The identities of the other informants have not been disclosed, and I can't help but consider some of Braithe's disappearing into undisclosed places. Is she in league with her sister?

"Isn't anyone going to say anything? Hello would be nice." Libby steps into the centre of the group, totally unafraid and confident in her own abilities.

I don't like the smile. It's not natural.

No one is really sure who Libby is anymore. I had been told that Romney was not to be trusted, but at this moment, I would have trusted her above Libby.

Grainne voices what everyone is thinking. "How did you get here?" Any one person would need another pair of hands to work the airlock controls.

"I borrowed one of the janitors and its scooter. It's not that far. Anyway, I've brought good news — for some. Not so good for others."

No one speaks, but all eyes are on her standing in the middle of the group.

"I've managed to patch a call through to an unmanned observation satellite. When Mars checks for updates they'll find it."

I can feel the tension relax within our group. The Caputa looks resigned, but Branchard looks furious. He had trusted Libby.

"With a bit of luck, we can rig up something more permanent once we've sorted this situation out. We can get a proper message to Mars explaining our position."

"You used my equipment?" Branchard seethes.

"Yes, my dear. I also told them that you were being held captive by a group of insurgents, along with the President of the UFP. Hopefully, that will get things moving. The President's name still means something, if I'm not mistaken."

"Oh, Libby." The voice was so quiet that I wonder if I'd heard it. "Why?" Noah asks, a little louder.

She looks puzzled for a minute and then smiles again. I decide that she has lost it. Romney had told me that she had been undercover for a long time. She allowed the death of her son. She is so screwed up that she has lost it.

She walks towards Branchard, and Jared makes to stop her. But, as he puts out a hand, she pulls a weapon from her pocket. He stops and looks hopelessly around as Libby begins to untie Branchard.

It is not the usual stun-gun, and the others are obviously fearful of it. I've seen them hanging by the cages of the Beasts. Laser-guns, ready in case one of them escapes. They are small for ease of carriage, but very deadly. Branchard is grinning from ear to ear and rubbing his wrists as he goes to release his sister.

I am watching their every move, terrified of what will happen next, but even so I am hard pressed to describe what does.

One minute, Branchard is bending over The Caputa attempting to untie her. Then both slump over, him falling to the floor as she falls across the table. Libby is still standing with the laser-gun hot in her hand, but before Noah reaches her, she turns it on herself.

The collective cry comes too late.

I TAP LIGHTLY on the door of Tadz's apartment, but it's Nan who opens it, not Tadz as I had hoped. She is still bruised, and the cuts, although healing, are red and angry. She hobbles back from the door to allow me in.

"How is he?" I ask.

Nobody other than Nan and I have seen Tadz since that dreadful day. He has taken Libby's death very badly, coming on top of Jaimz's. Marcie comes around to help Nan, and has done so since she first left the clinic, but he won't even see her. Nan is worried, and she has enough to cope with due to her own injuries. I have been trying to help them, but they have pretty much closed themselves off. At least Nan lets me and Marcie in with some necessities.

Nan ignores my query and greets me with one of her own. "What's happening out there?"

"It's slow going," I tell her. "People are still suspicious of Jared, so there's no real leadership and those in the Admin Domes aren't used to thinking for themselves."

"Noah not back, then?"

"Not yet. I wouldn't be in his shoes for the whole of the universe on a plate."

"Tea?" Nan indicates the kettle.

I nod. "Things are beginning to move. Romney and Jared are holding it together. They've made a good start."

"Dad always said that boy had hidden depths. This seems to be proving him right. How's Braithe?"

Libby and Braithe had had quite an argument, according to Romney, before Libby had attacked her sister and made her way to the PolliPauz.

"Not coping very well. Oh, she puts on a brave face, but soon makes an excuse to go back to her apartment. Romney's the only one she has much to do with. Libby's behaviour shocked her to her core. She's grieving for her and worried about Noah."

"I'm surprised she didn't go with him," Nan considers.

"I think she wanted to but was told to stay put by the Federation. But then, she wasn't there, was she? They say they're trying to prevent collusion."

"Too late for that — not that there is any. What happened, happened. You all saw it." Nan had switched the kettle on, but her right arm is broken, so I make the tea.

"How are you doing?" I ask her.

Nan insists she hadn't had an issue with the person who attacked her before that day. She thinks it was all in the heat of the moment when tempers were high and reason had gone out of the window.

"Slow but sure. I'm just glad to be out of the clinic. The pain relief was the only good thing about that place." She tries to grin, but it obviously hurts her. "It was all a bit — clinical," she attempts to joke.

I smile and add, "I know this is easy for me to say, but you must rest. Let me do the fetching and carrying for you."

"I wish Dad would let Mum look after him. She's more than willing, but he won't see anyone."

I don't say it, but I wish he would as well. I am happy to help; Nan is my friend and I'm very fond of Tadz. But it isn't strictly true that nothing much is happening. I've just said that to Nan so she doesn't feel bad about me helping her when there's so much to be done. It's slow work, but there's a lot going on behind the scenes, and I am heavily involved.

Most of my work is in the Admin Domes, and as Tadz and Nan are in Tadz's apartment in the Agricultural Dome, it means a long trek to and fro. I'm hoping to be moved nearer as the work moves on but I don't know when that will be.

With Noah away, and Tadz and Braithe grieving, Romney, Grainne and Jared have taken over as leads in the clear up, but Jared is mature enough to realize that they cannot authorize large changes without team approval, and by that I mean a team headed by Noah and Braithe. Besides, Jared is considered too young, and Romney is still regarded with suspicion. She was in the Admin Domes for a very long time, and rumours spread quicker than the truth.

It seems that the Controllers, on the say-so of Branchard, shut off all communication with Mars, so it's no wonder they thought we were all dead. Apparently, they did a good job of disabling the system, I just hope that it won't take too long to fix.

We are all waiting for Noah to get back. It's as if the whole of Ceres is holding its collective breath, waiting for the result of the Federation Review. The death of its President will not be taken lightly, and Noah will have to make them understand that no one could have foreseen the outcome or stopped it. There are those who think that he will be made a scapegoat and its upsetting morale. The Caputa was right when she said that the penalty for murder under the Federation is death. The human race has not had such a harsh penalty for hundreds of years, and are finding it abhorrent.

•   •   •

The arrival of Marcie with clean clothing for Tadz and Nan gives me the chance to make my escape. There are no laundry chutes and neatly folded clean clothes here. We have to do things very differently. Marcie sees to the cleaning of their apartment, as she lives nearby, and I make sure they have food and company.

I wonder how those in the Admin Domes will cope with the changes. We are so used to everything being automatic. The mono-pods run endlessly; you just jump on one as it idles by and get off as it drifts through your port. You drop the clothes you wore for the day into the laundry chute and open the drawer next to it, where clean ones appear by the magic of technology. At the moment, this is still happening, as nothing has yet been re-programmed. The clothing will not last forever, but a detail has been organized to deal with it.

The biggest change is the food.

Jared ordered the immediate clearance of the food silos. Romney insisted it all be buried as befitted human remains, so maintenance 'bots cleared a pit in the ice, and it was disposed of with due ceremony.

There were concerns that the inhabitants of the Admin Domes would suffer from withdrawal symptoms once the drugs were removed from food; stocks of the medications are available in order to wean people off. All appear groggy and disorientated, and we are making it known that the drugs are there. If we can help them get by, then they get by.

The silos have been blasted clean and are now being used to store fresh produce from the farms. It all needs preparing and freezing and then proper cooking before eating. Everything was automated before. The inhabitants of Domes 1 and 2 are in for a bit of a rude awakening and fast-track learning. No stopping by the Refectory and helping yourself to whatever takes your fancy. At the moment, they are having to make do with bread and cheese and some preserved fruit. There are plans afoot to cull some of the animals and use them for their meat, but we need to be sure we have sufficient breeding stock before we start that program.

There's a lot to do, and I need to get back to DN 1, so make my way to the food storage depot. Grainne is there as I had hoped, supervising a consignment of fresh produce ready for the Admin Domes.

"Hey Jax," she calls as she spots me. "What can I do for you?"

She looks cheerful enough, but there are lines on her face that were not there before the "Rising," as it's being called. She and her family are co-ordinating the supplies for the inhabited domes as well as working their own farm.

"I'm on my way to DN 1 and was wondering if there was any chance of a lift? I need to get to work and I'm already running late."

The food trucks drawn by maintenance 'bots travel at faster than jogging pace, and a lift on the back of one will save my legs as well as time.

"I've just finished loading this truck," she tells me, checking her technopad. "You can sit on top and get a ride back if you wish. It's going to DN 2. Is that alright?" I nod and make my way over. "How're Nan and Tadz?" she asks.

I shrug as I climb onto the wagon. "So-so."

She smiles wanly, "How are you?"

"So-so," I repeat, as the maintenance 'bot pulls away from the depot, the truck jerking behind. I cling on as we head for the tunnels, and turn and watch her as she waves the next truck into line.

'VE BEEN ASSIGNED to help organize the recovery of the
Industrial Domes, and once we have our immediate needs
successfully catered for, I shall take over that role full time.
Jared has an ambitious plan for the recovery of the domes in
order to make us independent, so that nothing like this ever
happens again.

I have an office, and a team beneath me, making me feel
nervous. I don't know if I'm cut out to be a leader, but Jared
seems to think so, and he's the one everyone is beginning to
turn to for direction. Noah still isn't back. I would have liked
to have been involved with the Agricultural Domes, as I was
beginning to feel at home there, but those who have been
living there are getting on top of that.

It is important that we get the Industrial Domes up and
running again. No one knows what will happen between us and
the Martian colony now they know we've survived. It will all

depend on the Federation's findings and ultimate decision. After two disastrous attempts at the colonization of Ceres, they may decide to cut their losses and formulate a different plan. If that is the case, there are commodities we will need if we are going to be a viable community with half a chance of surviving here.

I bump into BJ as I make my way from the storage silo in DN 2, where the food truck dropped me off. I am heading towards the mono-port as he is leaving it. He didn't remember me at all, so we've had to start again. I haven't mentioned the fact that we were destined to become connubial before all this happened. I doubt the Controllers' ideas of pairing us off will still stand, which is good because, although I'm growing to like this new BJ now that he's not doped up and is quite a bit slimmer, I wouldn't like to spend my whole life with him.

Food is not as plentiful as it used to be now that the farms are having to feed everyone. We'll not starve, and the food is healthy and nutritious, but we do have to be careful with portions, even with the modified strains that produce an abundant harvest.

"Hey Jax."

"Hey yourself."

"What are you doing?" he asks.

"I'm going to work. I've just been to see how my friend is. Nan, who was hurt in the "Rising." Is there anything I can do for you? Only I'm in a bit of a rush."

"No, it's alright. What time do you finish?"

"About eight tonight."

BJ looks about to say something when Justin Phillips, Grainne's eldest son, comes bouncing up. We've been working closely together and are getting along quite nicely, thank you. He's kind and thoughtful and makes me laugh. He's good with people and is assigned to getting together working parties with the right skills to repair the Industrial Domes and make them ready for use.

"Hi Jax. If you're on your way to work, I'll escort you." He gives a playful bow, a big daft grin on his face.

BJ takes a step backwards. "I'll perhaps see you later," he mumbles and disappears into the silo.

"A friend of yours?" Justin wants to know.

"Yes. A long-time friend as it happens." I don't mention the fact that we were to have been connubial. "From before the "Rising."

"And he remembers you?"

"No. We've had to get reacquainted."

"Anything I should know?"

"No," I say, and I don't even consider that I might have to cross my fingers. It's not a lie. What happened before the "Rising" stays before the "Rising."

There's a whole new world waiting to be explored.

ABOUT THE AUTHOR

Sue Eaton was a teacher of children with autism and special needs for many years, and has written drama for children with communication and social needs, earning a Millennium award. She has published a science fiction/historical novel, *The Woman Who Was Not His Wife*, and has had short stories published in four horror anthologies, one science fiction anthology, and has edited an anthology of ghost stories.

YOU MIGHT ALSO ENJOY

MEMORY AND METAPHOR
by Andrea Monticue

Civilization fell. It rose.
At some point, people built starships.

SNAIL'S PACE
by Susan McDonough-Wachtman

Orphaned and penniless in Hong Kong in 1884 — what's a young gentlewoman to do?

A WRECK OF DRAGONS
by Elaine Isaak

Teens and their giant robots search for a new home for mankind, but the planet they discover belongs to the dragons.

Available from Water Dragon Publishing in
hardcover, trade paperback, and digital editions
waterdragonpublishing.com